Love Hurts

Accelerated Reader Information
as provided by www.arbookfind.com

Interest Level (suggested maturity level):
UG (high school)

Book Level: _3.8_   AR Test: _4.0_ **pts.**

Love Rules

Love Hurts

Beverly Scudamore

James Lorimer & Company Ltd., Publishers
Toronto

James Lorimer & Company Ltd., Publishers acknowledges the support of the Ontario Arts Council. We acknowledge the financial support of the Government of Canada through the Canada Book Fund for our publishing activities. We acknowledge the support of the Canada Council for the Arts which last year invested $24.3 million in writing and publishing throughout Canada. We acknowledge the Government of Ontario through the Ontario Media Development Corporation's Ontario Book Initiative.

Cover image: Shutterstock
Cover design: Meredith Bangay

Library and Archives Canada Cataloguing in Publication
Scudamore, Beverly, 1956-
    Love hurts / Beverly Scudamore.

(SideStreets)
Issued also in an electronic format.
ISBN 978-1-4594-0367-3 (bound). — ISBN 978-1-4594-0366-6 (pbk.)

    I. Title. II. Series: SideStreets

PS8587.C82L68 2013   jC813'.54   C2012-907828-X

James Lorimer & Company Ltd.,   Distributed in the United States by:
Publishers   Orca Book Publishers
317 Adelaide Street West, Suite #1002   P.O. Box 468
Toronto, ON, Canada   Custer, WA U.S.A.
M5V 1P9   98240-0468
www.lorimer.ca

Printed and bound in Canada.
Manufactured by Webcom in Toronto, Ontario, Canada in February 2013.
Job #398018

For Susan

Chapter 1

I'm late for school and all I want to do is close my eyes and drift back to sleep, listening to my iPod. Last night, I lay awake in bed, obsessing about Dustin Williams. We're in grade eleven together and he's my best guy friend. Our "friendship" is the problem. I want more . . . but — sigh — no. He keeps making it clear that he doesn't want a romantic relationship, and I keep hanging on, hoping he'll change his mind. Some might consider that loyal . . . or maybe pathetic.

Bam! A heavy-metal tune jolts me like an electric shock. Yikes! I must have drifted off again. Now I'm really late. I rush out of bed, down a glass of grape juice, and plug in my hair straightener. I'm getting the kinks out of my long, brown hair and forcing my side bangs to behave when my best friend, Peyton Lane, texts me. It's about her latest boyfriend problem. Her daily dramas are way more exciting than anything that happens in my life. This latest one, about her boyfriend and his so-called "study partner," does not disappoint. Unfortunately, I have to cut our conversation short.

I rush to the elevator and then stand there waiting, pressing the button. It finally arrives and I go down sixteen floors. Snow is still falling from last night's blizzard. A blast of cold air slaps my face. Since I'm running late, I decide to take the shortcut through the park. Turns out, it's a bad idea: the snow is up to my knees. I try running, powering my Uggs through the drifts, but tire out quickly. By the time I reach the back of the football field, the bell rings.

Ahead, the reserve bus pulls into the roundabout at the side of the school. The Aamjiwnaang First Nation reserve is just south of the city. Their bus must have been delayed in the snow. I watch the students pile out and head to the entrance. Dustin and his little buddy, Ben, are the last two off. Dustin is tall and muscular with dark hair and eyes. Ben is in grade nine. He's short and wiry and looks like he's in grade five. If it weren't for Dustin, I wouldn't notice him.

"Dustin!" I call, running up to him.

He cracks a smile. "Hey, Mel! Late again?"

"Like clockwork," I reply, laughing.

While I'm talking to Dustin, Ben heads for the side door. Suddenly, he yells, "Fight!" and starts running.

Dustin and I follow to check out the action.

8

Two guys are shouting and going at it hard in the snow. I recognize one of them: a grade ten football player. The other one is smaller and he's taking a bad beating. The football player punches him in the gut, making him double over in pain. As soon as he straightens up — wham! — a fist slams into the side of his head. He slumps, looking dazed. Raising his hands to his head, he tries to protect himself.

"Leave him alone!" I scream, waving my arms. "He's half your size!"

The big guy doesn't listen, so I throw my back-pack at them. No effect. I nudge Dustin. "Do something!"

He gives me a look. "Umm . . . I'm not sure . . ."

"Get in there!" I insist, pushing him.

He scowls at me, then tosses his coat and back-pack and walks into the middle of the scrum. Grabbing the football player from behind, Dustin locks his arms around the guy's chest, ripping his shirt. The weaker kid took this as his chance to escape into the school. Meanwhile, they tee-ter and fall off balance, thrashing around on the ground — but not for long. Dustin is six feet tall and a competitive wrestler; the other guy is big in attitude, but a lightweight, and no match for Dustin. With one smooth move, Dustin puts him in a martial arts hold, his thumb applying pressure to the back of the guy's arm. Right now, an exquisite kind of pain will be shooting up a nerve. I smile, knowing how much it hurts.

Just then, the principal, Mrs. Franklin, storms out of the school. She's marching like a military soldier, wearing a forest green skirt and matching blazer. Her grey-brown hair is pulled back in a tight bun.

I grab Dustin. "Quick, let's get outta here."

We make a beeline for the rear entrance. After we enter the school, we slow to a normal walk. He elbows me and grins. "Nice move."

"Huh?"

"The backpack — very scary."

I punch his shoulder and we laugh. He puts his arm around me and we head to our lockers. He's sweaty, but I don't mind.

"You okay?" he asks, giving me a little squeeze. "You're trembling."

"That was a lot of blood," I admit. "If you hadn't been here, that kid would have been destroyed."

"The big guy was really worked up," he says. "Thought the other guy had been hitting on his girlfriend."

Unfortunately, our conversation gets interrupted. *She* approaches quickly, walking with purpose. "I've been looking for you."

Stalking is more like it, I'm thinking.

Dustin's arm falls away as we step apart. Gina Rondelli slides in between us, grabbing his hand. "I was worried," she says in a high, breathy tone, ". . . with the snow and all."

"Oh, gag," I cough under my breath.

She gives me a withering stare. "Don't you have class?"

"Yep. And you?"

"I got excused to go to the washroom."

Since school just started, I'm tempted to ask, *Leaky bladder?* But I hold my tongue and walk away, forcing myself to remain civilized.

Gina is beautiful but only on the outside. She's got long, black hair and big brown eyes. She's ridiculously skinny, except for her massive boobs. Skinny girl + gigantic breasts = surgery. It's not just speculation; she brags about her boob job. She says she went from 34A to 38D. Am I jealous? Yes, but only cuz she's with Dustin. She's syrupy sweet to him, but it won't last. One day, he's going to realize that Gina is all about Gina. The girls see through her. All the guys see is rubber boobs.

If only Dustin would look at me that way.

Reality check: NOT GOING TO HAPPEN. I'm pretty sure it's wrong to crush on the same guy for over a year when he's made it clear he's not interested. I have to face it and get on with my life.

Problem is: I don't want to.

Chapter 2

At the office, I wait in line to pick up a late slip. When I finally make it to the secretary's desk, Ms. Sanchez looks up in surprise. "Mel Rankin, what a coincidence! I was about to page you from class. The principal would like a word with you."

"I'm just late," I explain.

"Take a chair, please. She won't be long."

Weird, I'm thinking. *A late detention is not a big deal.*

I sit on one of the chairs lined against the wall. Eventually, the office clears and it's just me and Ms. Sanchez. She's staring at the computer. Every now and then, her eyes widen. Who knew the office computer held such drama? Then again, a lot of crazy stuff does happen at Meridian High. Bored, I play with my hair, twirling it around my fingers and checking for split ends.

A guy I've never seen enters the office. Hmmm

. . . this is interesting! My eyes lock on, following him to the secretary's desk. He's tall and wearing a blue-and-yellow-striped rugby shirt. His worn jeans fit just right, riding low on his lean hips. A backpack is slung over his shoulder. His brown hair falls below his ears in short layers. Nice — I like a guy with hair. This guy is new. And hot.

Just the thing to help me get over Dustin, I'm thinking. Not seriously, but he *is* hard to ignore.

When he's telling Ms. Sanchez his name — Colter Wagner — I'm finger-combing my hair. When he's filling out a form, I'm applying lip gloss. When she's handing him some papers and telling him to take a seat, I'm shifting my eyes to the floor. I stop breathing when I see boots. I look up. An entire empty room and he selects the chair next to me!

He smiles at me, and I immediately notice his striking eyes: light brown with flecks of gold. My cheeks flush and I smile back.

Extending his hand, he says, "Hey, I'm Colter."

"Mel," I say, awkwardly placing my hand in his. Our handshake lingers; his grasp feels like a warm caress.

"Waiting to see the principal?" he asks.

Tongue-tied, I manage to nod.

"Me too. She's in the cafeteria talking to a cop."

"There was a fight," I offer.

"Yeah, I figured it was something like that. Were you involved? That why you're here?"

"What? No! I watched . . . that's all."

"Didn't think so," he says, grinning. "You don't look like a tough chick."

Tossing my hair over my shoulder, I quip, "I'm usually pretty tame." Immediately, I want to kick myself. My flirting is sooo obvious. Next time I open my mouth, I tone it down. "Are you new? I haven't seen you around."

"First day," he groans.

"Ouch . . . been there, done that, a couple of years ago. Sarnia is pretty decent, except there are no hills — all this snow and not a blip. Sucks after growing up in Calgary and boarding at Sunshine and Lake Louise. But the summers make up for it. Sarnia has amazing beaches and badass outdoor concerts at Bayfest."

I suddenly get the feeling he's not listening. He's looking over my shoulder, beyond me. I turn to see what's got his attention, and there's Dustin. His eyes are shifting from me to Colter, like he's trying to figure out what's going on.

"Why are you here?" I ask Dustin.

"Beats me . . . I got called down."

"Do you think it's about the fight? Cuz, like, we're sooo not involved."

He gives me a look, a reminder that I pushed him right into the middle of it.

"We couldn't just stand there!" I insist.

I'm about to introduce Colter when Ms. Sanchez says, "Dustin Williams, the principal will see you now."

"I was here first!" I pipe up, half-heartedly.

Actually, I don't mind sticking around and getting to know Colter. For the next few minutes, we talk about *me*. It feels odd but nice. When I'm with my best friend, Peyton, we usually talk about *her*. When I'm with Dustin, he talks about the Leafs and Xbox. I tell Colter about my dog, Chevy — how I miss him like crazy — and how it sucks living more than three thousand kilometres away from my family. I'm showing him the bend in my baby finger, where I dislocated it playing volleyball, when Dustin walks out. His eyes are daggers.

Alarmed, I stand up.

"What a load of crap."

Before I can ask why, Mrs. Franklin appears at the open doorway. "Miss Rankin, you may come in now."

She sits across from me at her desk, shuffling papers, as if I'm not there. When she looks up, she's frowning. "During this morning's assault, I noticed that you and Mr. Williams left rather quickly."

"We were late for school," I say, shifting uncomfortably.

"The two of you broke school rules. You witnessed the incident and Dustin participated."

"It's not like that," I explain. "Neither of us knew who was fighting or why. We weren't even there when it broke out. If Dustin hadn't stopped the fight —"

She interrupts me: "Joe Simmons's shirt was

ripped. Clearly Dustin used excessive force. And the martial arts move —"

"Joe was the problem!" I insist, my voice rising. "Not Dustin. Anyway, he has used that hold on me before. It's not a big deal."

Her eyes turn into saucers. "On school property?"

"We were fooling around!" As soon as the words are out, I'm guessing she will twist *that* too.

She clasps her hands firmly on the desk. "Right now, I am concerned with the part *you* played in this morning's events. Meridian High's rules are laid out clearly. If you see a fight, you must report it to the office. By hanging around and watching, you encourage fighting."

I shake my head in disbelief. "You think I was cheering them on?"

She nods. "For your part in this morning's events, a corrective action is appropriate."

If I wasn't so angry, I'd laugh. I've been found guilty in a kangaroo court.

Chapter 3

Corrective action. I have no idea what that means, but it doesn't sound good. When I find out it involves physical labour, I stare at Mrs. Franklin in horror. "Are you serious?"

"Studies show that suspensions don't work," she explains. "Students tend to watch television or visit the mall. You are one of the first to join a new program we hope will take the fun out of the day. Mr. Jenkins has prepared a list of odd jobs around the school." Pulling out a notebook, she reads: "Clean the bottoms of the chairs in Gym B." A little smile creeps onto her face. "Off you go. Mr. Jenkins will give you what you need."

I storm out of the office and head straight for the washrooms. Standing in front of a sink, I make a face at myself in the mirror. My blue eyes are raging. *How dare she? Everyone knows what's on the bottom of those chairs: old chewing gum. Some of the mouths at Meridian should be illegal: bad breath . . . food in braces . . . cavities . . . disease . . .*

I drop my head over the sink and moan, "I feel like puking."

"Get a toilet. Not cool on the floor."

I whirl around. When did that grade twelve girl walk in? "I'm — uh — not actually going to . . ."

"Good," she says, tying back her dreadlocks.

I trudge down the hall to Mr. Jenkins's office. I explain my situation, and he offers a sympathetic smile. "Good thing I didn't put the chairs away after the senior band concert last night. That should save you some trouble." Heading to the supply closet, he grabs a chisel, rubber gloves, and a can of WD-40. "Good luck," he says with a shrug. "The dang stuff is like superglue. If you need more tools, come visit me again."

"Thanks," I mutter. I should be nicer to him. After all, it's not his fault.

Gym B doubles as an auditorium at Meridian High. When I enter, I see five hundred chairs arranged in rows from last night's concert.

How bad can it be? I tell myself. I mean, how many high-school kids actually stick gum on the bottoms of chairs? That is sooo immature.

The first chair I check has two grey blobs stuck to the bottom. The next is worse. I count six wads, hard and cracked — ancient offerings. That's when I realize the bottoms of the chairs have never been cleaned. Uck! I make a mental note: *never touch the bottom of a chair again.*

Grasping the chisel, I chip away at a big hunk, only to find it's stuck like cement. I'm getting nowhere, so I go on to the next. One good smack and it flies off, hitting me in the eye — and sending me running back to the washroom. When I return, I shove the chisel into a pink blob and it sinks in. A fresh wad! Pulling my hand back, the gum stretches in a stringy mess between the chair and the chisel. I try to kick the chair loose but miss and hit air.

When I look up, I see Colter standing in the doorway, grinning. I must look psycho, so I try to explain my situation. He laughs, revealing a dimple on his left cheek. And I find myself laughing too.

"Why are you here?" I ask, putting the chisel down.

"Lost." He holds up a timetable. "I'm supposed to be in room 217."

"Can I see?" My eyes glance over his schedule. "We have Art together," I note, smiling.

"Sick," he says, like he means it.

"It really sucks being the new kid," I say. "My family transferred from Calgary when I was halfway through grade nine. The worst part of the day is lunch with a room full of strangers."

"Gee, thanks, I feel better now."

"Ouch! Sorry." I throw my hand over my mouth. "You can eat at my table."

He doesn't reply. Why should he? I'm acting like such a loser. "I'll take you to room 217," I say.

"You'll never find it on your own. This school was built to confuse students."

He gives a little shrug. "I've already missed most of first period. If you want, I could help you with the chairs."

Before he can change his mind, I hand him the chisel and say, "Go for it."

While Colter chips away at the hard pieces of gum, I spray WD-40 on the fresh, gooey stuff. At lunch, we buy snacks from the vending machine and eat together on the auditorium stage. It was Colter's idea — he says he hates cafeteria food. I'm thinking: *Vending-machine food?* But he's helping me out, so I don't argue. A chance meeting in the office, and here we are a couple of hours later, gone from total strangers to friends . . . and maybe more. In a strange way, I have Mrs. Franklin to thank for this. The crazy chaos of the morning has brought us together. Looks like her "tough love" backfired. Too bad, Mrs. F, you didn't take the fun out of my day, after all.

Chapter 4

The place where I live doesn't feel like home. For the past five months, I've been living with my aunt Stella. She acts like I don't exist, which leaves me pretty much on my own. Her whole world is her job as an executive secretary, shopping for designer bargains, and her date of the week — the man who is supposed to change her life but ends up another disappointment. There are benefits to my living arrangement: Aunt Stella won't care about the "corrective action" notice. She'll sign it and say something like, "Better luck next time, kiddo."

It's hard to believe that she and my mom are sisters. If Mom found out what happened, she'd go into major lecture mode, yakking on and on — and I'd be going "la, la, la" in my head, trying to tune her out. At sixteen, I want my parents off my back, but I don't want to be completely ignored. Right from the start, I knew Aunt Stella was not parent material. I figured she'd be like a big sister, looking out for me and hanging out. I imagined shopping sprees and late-night movies and lots of girl talk. What I got is a big, empty void.

Aunt Stella lives in a two-bedroom apartment on the sixteenth floor of a high-rise overlooking the St. Clair River. Her place is finished in three colours: red, black, and white. Since my bedroom decor ruins her perfect colour scheme, she insists I keep my door shut. My stuffed dolphin and a coconut with a painted face sit next to my computer. On the wall is a poster of Luke Bryan at his spring-break concert. A blow-up palm tree sits in a corner. No matter how hard I try, the red walls murder my tropical theme.

If Dad hadn't gotten laid off last summer, my family would still be together. When he got the news, Mom had just graduated with an Environmental Technology diploma. She tried but couldn't find work in Sarnia. When she got offered a one-year contract with an environmental firm in Fort McMurray, Alberta, she thought about moving on her own for the short time. But then, Suncor Energy, a major oil company, offered Dad work. His new job — driving a truck at the oil sands — would pay big bucks.

Suddenly, the whole family was moving. My younger sister, Lori, was pumped about living close to the best ski hills in the country. Not me. I had just gone through the trauma of switching high schools a year and a half earlier — figuring out the people to get close to and the ones to stay away from . . . finding a place where I fit. I wasn't going through that again if I could help it. But then, my cool aunt Stella — who I didn't know that well but who had bought me real Uggs for Christmas — offered to take me for the year. It seemed like a no-brainer.

***

After school, I flop on the couch, daydreaming about my crazy day. I like Colter. He's lots of fun and good with a chisel. And . . . he keeps my mind off Dustin.

Peyton texts me. " r u home???"
"yes"
"need to talk. be right over"

Ten minutes later, I buzz her up. Her red hair is cut in layers. When I met her in grade nine, she had black hair, but she swears her hair is naturally blond. Her roots look brown to me. So . . . whatever.

We sprawl out on my bed. "Where were you at lunch?" she asks, pouting. "I needed to talk."

She doesn't wait for my reply, so I can tell her about *my* day. Instead, she starts going off about *her* problems. I already know most of the story from her "distress" texts this morning. Her boyfriend, Chad, went for study help with a girl named Rachael the night before. But then, a friend of Peyton's saw them together at Tim Hortons. She told Peyton that the two were whispering and giggling, with no books in sight. When Peyton asked Chad about it, all he said was "I wanted a doughnut."

Peyton is fired up and ranting in my ears, but I'm not listening. For once, I want it to be about me. She jabs my shoulder with her finger. "Tell me what you think?" She's demanding an answer to something. What — I have no idea.

"That's crazy," I say absently.

She narrows her eyes at me. "You weren't listening!"

Busted, I make an attempt to listen. First break in the conversation, I try to tell her about Colter, but she switches the subject back to Chad. Frustrated, I get up and leave.

"What's your problem?" she calls after me.

"I'm going to make Kraft Mac."

Peyton is just being Peyton. I'm the one not acting like myself. She follows me to the kitchen. "Tell me about the guy you met," she says, finally cluing in.

Looking up from the pot, I smile. Now that I have her attention, I talk while we're waiting for the water to boil.

Leaning on the kitchen counter, she tilts her head. "Are you saying you're over Dustin?"

"Me . . . over Dustin? Seriously, Peyton, the world couldn't change that much in one day.

There's something between us. It's hard to explain."

"Gina is what's between the two of you," she points out.

"Ouch," I say, flicking the spoon at her. "Don't mention her name!"

"Seriously, Mel, you need a guy who's into you — and you only. Dustin is a jerk for leading you on."

"He doesn't," I insist. "Not on purpose anyway. He just doesn't get it yet."

"Get what?"

I empty the macaroni into the boiling water, then look up with a dreamy smile. "That we should be together."

She groans loudly. "Oh, boy, you really need to move on."

"You're right." I sigh. "It's just hard."

"So where is Colter from?" she asks.

"Uhhh . . ." I try to remember, but can't.

Peyton gives me a weird look. "You spent the whole day with him. Isn't that the first thing you ask someone new?"

"We talked about other stuff."

"What do you know about this mystery man?"

"He's got a dimple right here," I say, poking her left cheek.

"You do like him," she says, waggling a finger at me.

"The macaroni's ready," I say, grabbing two bowls. We hang out until five, watching *Ellen* and

Dr. Oz. Later, I go on the computer to chat with Dustin, but he's offline. Unlike my other friends, he doesn't spend much time on his computer. He'd rather play Xbox Call of Duty. Since I didn't see him all day, I call his cell to compare punishments. Turns out, he spent the day removing scuff marks from the halls. We agree I got the nastier job.

At eight o'clock, I log in to my Facebook chat. My profile picture is my dog, Chevy. He's a shepherd/corgi mix, a big dog packed into a little body. This is the time I usually talk to Mom, since it's five o'clock out there, and she's home from work. As usual, she asks about my day. When I omit the part about slaving in the gym and meeting a new guy (too many questions), there's not a lot to tell. After we say goodbye, I stare at my computer, thinking, *Should I?*

Creeping on Colter's Facebook is sort of crossing a line, but Peyton got me curious: Where *does* he come from? Before I know it, my fingers go to work and, just like that, his page pops up. One album is open to the public.

A quick click and the screen shows rows of photos. I am not prepared for what I see. "What the?" I say to his smiling profile picture. "You've got a girlfriend."

She's in every picture. Her name is Jillian Ward. I know this because she's tagged on a couple of photos. She has long, cinnamon hair and side bangs that sweep over her eyes. Same hairstyle as me. Her blue eyes sparkle, and the tiny freckles on her nose and cheeks give her a sunny glow. Some photos are just of her. But in others, she's posing with Colter. They are embracing at a concert, gazing into each other's eyes at the junior prom, dressed in school colours at their homecoming . . . There are no pictures of his guy friends and no embarrassing party pictures.

This doesn't make sense. Why did he spend the whole day with me? Was he was just being friendly? . . . cuz it felt like more. I'm about to shut down his page when I notice something: the school he attends is listed as Ryder High. That's in Sarnia, on the other side of town. When he said he was new, I assumed he was from a different city. And he didn't correct me when I was blabbing on about Sarnia. Peyton's right: this guy is a mystery. Why would he transfer in January? Did he get kicked out? Is he picking up a course not offered at his school? Or . . . is it something else?

Whatever, I don't care.

I shut down the computer, crawl under the covers, and hug my pillow. It's too early to fall asleep, but I don't feel like doing anything.

My life sucks. In addition to my aunt being absent, my closest friends are in relationships. I don't even have my little sister to bug. It was just over a year ago when Dustin and I were together at a party. The house was getting out of control and kids were hanging around the front yard, yelling and making a scene. It was only time before the cops would arrive. Not wanting any trouble,

Dustin and I split and went for a walk. Wandering through a park on that snowy night, we kissed under the full moon. That's when we finally admitted our feelings went beyond friendship. The pieces of my life were coming together in a perfect fit — except for one detail: my boyfriend, Travis. He was out of town that weekend at a hockey tournament, and I didn't want to hurt him — not like that. So the next day, I told Dustin the kiss had been a mistake and that I was not going to break up with Travis. That's when he said, "Is it because I'm from the reserve?"

I told him, "Of course not," but the hurt look on his face made me wonder if he believed me. He's sensitive about things like that, probably because he's had to deal with some of the racist kids at school.

After that, Dustin and I remained friends, but it was never the same. Even though I tried, I couldn't stop thinking about that kiss and wanting more. When he started dating Gina Rondelli, I was crushed. What happened next is a classic high-school tragedy. A month later, I caught Travis making out with some girl at a party. If only I had been true to my heart, Dustin and I would have had a chance.

I still want that chance.

Chapter 5

In the morning, the apartment is strangely quiet, so I go and knock on Aunt Stella's bedroom door. When she doesn't answer, I turn the handle and peek in. The fancy pillows are stacked high into a fountain of white silk on her bed. There is no sign of her. Did she even come home last night? Her lifestyle is none of my business, but I do need her to sign my "corrective action" note from the office.

When I arrive at school, I stop at the cafeteria to buy a banana muffin for breakfast. Sarah Binder is there ordering a coffee. We sit together and talk about volleyball. Sarah's parents are from India, but she was born in Canada. She isn't in a relationship, and it feels good to talk about something other than boys. I wish we could hang out more, but she's working two part-time jobs, trying to save money for university. It doesn't leave much free time.

Sarah and I are heading to class when I see him. He's wearing a T-shirt that reveals a nice set of muscles. I really wish Colter didn't look so good. If I could, I'd escape down a hall, but there is no exit.

"Hey, glad I found you," he says, walking up to us. "I never did figure out where my first class is."

I want to say, "Get lost," but I'm too nice. I turn to Sarah and say, "Go ahead. I'll see you in class." Spinning on my heels, I break into a fast walk. "Hurry, I've got five minutes to get to one end of the building and back."

"It's too early to run," he says, jogging to keep up. "If you're going to be late cuz of me, let's skip first period."

"Very funny," I say, rolling my eyes.

"My car's in the parking lot. We could go somewhere."

Suddenly, I realize he's being serious. "Uhh . . . not a good idea," I say. "I've had too many lates already." What I'm thinking is: *Not cool hitting on me behind your girlfriend's back*. Only I can't say this without telling him I was creeping on his Facebook.

I drop Colter at his classroom and don't see him again until last period. Mr. Passingham, the Art teacher, is super popular. He refers to the classroom as his "studio," and he praises his students' artwork as if they were masterpieces. The metal work tables are arranged in a circle. Mr. Passingham works at a revolving easel in the middle.

He believes the circle connects our thoughts and sparks creativity.

When I enter the classroom, Colter is already seated. From across the room, he motions me to sit next to him. I respond with a hands-up shrug, and then slide onto the stool next to Dustin.

"Hey, Mel," he says, looking up from the drawing he started yesterday.

Our assignment was to sketch something that has deep, personal meaning. Dustin is working on a First Nations boy. There is a smile on one side of his face, tears on the other. Dustin always comes up with thoughtful drawings. He's tough on the outside, but once you get to know him, he is sensitive and caring. He volunteers at the youth drug counselling centre on the reserve, and I'm guessing the boy in the picture is someone he's met.

When Mr. Passingham walks by, he stops and observes the wildflower I'm working on. "Beautiful," he remarks. "What does it mean to *your* life?"

"I'm drawing the flower in protest of winter," I explain.

He stands there, staring at my work. "Perhaps you — uh — misunderstood the goal of the lesson. We're using art as a form of therapy."

I put down my charcoal pencil. "This is therapy. I'm sick of winter."

"You and me both!" he chuckles. "The sun hasn't peeked through the clouds in days. But I'm looking for something a little deeper. Often people

31

have a hard time putting words to their feelings, and they get bottled up inside. Picture a can of Pepsi. Now shake it."

"Okayyy . . ." I say, waiting for the punchline. But it doesn't come. Guess I'm supposed to figure it out myself.

"Drawing allows you to see your feelings," he goes on. "It can be part of the healing process."

I respond with a blank look. "Uh . . . I don't have *those* kinds of problems."

Mr. Passingham won't give up. "Perhaps you're not ready to express your emotions in an actual drawing. Let's try something different. Close your eyes and imagine the colour that best expresses how you feel."

"Red," I say, for no particular reason.

"Good. Now grab your paints and try putting your red feelings on paper. Just let your hands take over."

"No actual picture?"

"Just real and raw emotion in any form you like."

I eye him suspiciously. "Is this being marked?"

He shakes his head. "That would go against what I am trying to achieve."

"Okay . . . whatever."

When he leaves, I nudge Dustin. "A whole day's work wasted." I roll up my wildflower picture and toss it in the recycling bin.

When I've mixed fresh watercolours, I dip my brush in a bright red tone and put it on the paper, letting my hand take over like Mr. Passingham suggested. Nothing happens. A stain grows under my brush. This is dumb. At least it doesn't count for anything. I stare at the paper for a long time. Then, strangely enough, my hand starts moving — kind of like what happens on a Ouija board, which I never could figure out. It moves slowly in loops, big and small, around and around like the coils of a Slinky. The circular motion is hypnotic. At first, it's interesting, almost fun, but I have to wonder, *Why am I doing this?* Once the canvas is filled, I start a new one and find my hand drawing the same circles. Out of nowhere, my throat starts to swell. My eyes tear up. I look up and breathe.

Dustin yanks my ponytail. "You okay?"

"Yes."

But I'm not okay. Whatever just happened did not feel good. When class is over, I rush out the door, wanting to be alone.

"What's up?" Dustin asks, running to catch up. "You get in touch with some big, bad emotion?"

"Yeah, anger! I liked my flower."

Next thing I know, Colter is walking beside us. "S'up?" he says to Dustin. "We met yesterday in the office."

Dustin grunts. (It takes him a while to warm up to people.)

"So . . ." Colter goes on. "Are you two together?"

There's a flash in Dustin's eyes. "We're friends — that's all." Without another word, Dustin steps away from us, saying, "Gotta get my bus. Later."

Don't go, I'm thinking. But he does, and I'm left standing there with Colter.

"Wanna come to the Bulk Store?" he asks. "I'm craving fuzzy peaches."

Before I can say no, the scent of wild berry perfume hits my nose. Peyton butts in between us and introduces herself as "Mel's BFF." "Personally, I like sour gummies. Thinking of them makes my mouth water." Her bubbly, in-your-face attitude can be a bit overwhelming when you first meet her.

"You can come too . . . if you want," he says.

Peyton doesn't register the cool tone in his invitation. "Yes!" she cries, pumping the air with her fist.

Colter raises an eyebrow at her, then turns to me. "Are you in?"

"Umm . . . I've got a ton of homework after my 'corrective action' day."

Peyton shoots me a look. "Mel, we're talking about candy, not a weekend in Toronto! You'll have plenty of time for homework."

She's putting me in a difficult spot, but then, she doesn't know what I discovered on Facebook. "Okay," I say. "I'll go for a bit."

"Meet me at my car in five," Colter says. "It's the silver Mazda parked in the last row."

"Sweet!" Peyton shrieks. "We don't have to take the bus!"

As we head to our lockers, she grabs my arm. "He's cute . . . he's got a car . . . and he's sooo into you."

"Think again," I respond with a grimace.

34

She stops in the middle of the hall and pulls me around to face her. "What do you mean? The whole time we were talking, his eyes were locked on you."

"I creeped on his Facebook last night," I tell her.

She leans in real close. "What did you find?"

"Nineteen pictures of his girlfriend, Jillian. He's crazy about her. And . . . get this . . . she lives in Sarnia! Colter transferred from Ryder High."

For once, Peyton is speechless, but she recovers quickly. "He's a guy — they don't always update their profiles."

"Something happened in Art class," I whisper.

Her eyes widen. "Really? Did he make a move?"

"What? No! We did art therapy to uncover our deep feelings. I drew circles."

"Okayyy . . . you're telling me this because . . ."

"I finally get it!" I exclaim. "I'm going nowhere with Dustin. Starting right now, it's official: I'm giving up on him."

Peyton hugs me. "Good for you. Now you're free to consider someone new."

"Not so fast," I say, reading her mind. "With Colter, I'd start drawing triangles. Him, Jillian, and me."

"Honestly, Mel, you're talking in geometry. It doesn't have to be that complicated. Colter invited both of us to the Bulk Store. What's the harm?"

"I don't get it," I say. "He asked Dustin if we were going out. Why would he do that if he wasn't interested?"

"Now it's your turn," she says. "Ask him if he has a girlfriend. If he says yes, walk away."

"I can't just ask him," I say, making a face. "It would be too weird."

"Not for me. I'll ask."

"Seriously?" I say, considering the possibility.

Peyton is such a good friend. One way or another, the drama will end at the Bulk Store.

Chapter 6

Colter's Mazda has black leather seats and a sound system that thumps the air. The roads are still slushy from yesterday's snowstorm when we pull out of the school parking lot. Peyton is singing along with the music, so I don't have to worry about making conversation. When we arrive at the Bulk Store, we head to the candy aisle. An intense hunger is gnawing at the pit of my stomach. Or maybe I'm worried about what's going to happen next. When Colter reaches for a bag from the dispenser, Peyton and I exchange knowing looks.

"I'm craving chocolate," I announce, taking off to the far end of the store. As I'm selecting two large chunks of Belgian chocolate, my heart is pounding. I wonder what she's saying to him — and what he's saying back. Next I go to the nut aisle and fill a bag with almonds. As I'm reaching for a twist tie, a hand grabs me from behind.

"He doesn't have a girlfriend," Peyton whispers.

"Then what's up with the Facebook chick?" I ask suspiciously.

"How should I know? I couldn't exactly ask. Anyway, he likes you. He told me so."

My cheeks flush. "Are you sure?"

"Yesss! I wouldn't make something like that up."

I have to admit, this *is* getting interesting. The timing for a new relationship is perfect. When we return to the car, Peyton asks Colter to drop her off so she can babysit her little sister — a convenient excuse so we can be alone. Peyton loves to play matchmaker.

When it's just the two of us, Colter gives me one of his dimply smiles. "Wanna go to my place? I'll share my candy."

"Yumm . . ." I say, nodding.

"I bought you something." He passes me a bag that he had hidden in his coat pocket.

"Gum . . . gross!" Laughing, I toss it back at him.

As we drive to his house, I'm remembering that I didn't shower or put on any makeup this morning. When I got out of bed, I was in such a lousy mood that I simply tossed my hair into a messy ponytail. How could I have known I'd be going on a first date?

A few minutes later, we drive into a quiet cul-de-sac and pull up in front of a large stone bungalow with a three-car garage. "Most likely my dad is home," Colter says as we walk up to the entrance. We stop at the double doors with the lion-head knocker. "Before we go in, you should know that my dad's kind of messed up. He's a bigshot lawyer, but you'd never know it these days. He spends most of the time in the basement, doped up. Doubt you'll meet him . . . but in case you do, you've been warned."

"Oh . . . that's not good," I say, grimacing. "How'd he get like that . . . on second thought, it's none of my business."

"It's okay," Colter says. "He fell down the stairs and hurt his back. The doctor prescribed oxycodone for the pain. A couple of prescriptions later, he was addicted. Now the doctor has stopped supplying him, and he has to score his drugs other ways."

"Oh . . . I see," I say, imagining his street sources. "That must be hard on you and your mom."

"Not her problem," he says, stone-faced. "When things got rough, she bailed and went to sunny Florida. No warning. She didn't even say goodbye."

"Oh . . . that's far away."

"Farther the better," he mutters as he puts the key in the front door.

I don't understand: better for Colter or his mother? I get the feeling there's something he's not telling me, but I don't want to get too personal. After all, we barely know each other. But I feel bad for him. Neither of his parents is there for him.

I know how that feels — but at least mine can be reached on the phone.

Inside, we head to the kitchen, where I'm surrounded by gleaming granite countertops and dark wooden cabinets. The place is super clean — no dishes in the sink, not even a wet dishcloth. Colter and I sit on stools at the kitchen island and I place my Bulk Store bags on the counter.

"Those are big chunks of chocolate," he observes. "How do you eat them without dislocating your jaw?"

"I melt them to make almond bark."

"Sounds good . . . what are we waiting for?"

I give a little shrug. "I was going to make it later. But sure, why not?"

I melt the chocolate in the microwave and stir in the almonds. Then I pour the warm mixture on a cookie sheet and pop it in the fridge. While we're waiting for the bark to harden, we eat fuzzy peaches.

The living room and kitchen share one big, open space. Three black leather couches and a coffee table sit in front of a stone fireplace. A white shag carpet lies across the dark hardwood floors. The first time I see the rug move, I think my eyes are playing tricks on me. Then I realize a white dog is crouched under the table.

"Your dog matches the rug! She's so cute! What's her name?"

"Pixie."

I try calling her. She doesn't budge. "Why

didn't she greet us at the door? Bark . . . or do something?"

"She doesn't like strangers."

I walk over and kneel on the rug. At the same time, she slips deeper under the table. "Pixie," I call softly. Reaching under, I pet her trembling body.

"Come meet my other pet," Colter says. "He's friendly."

"What kind?" I ask, getting up and following.

He doesn't answer, and there are no stairs to hint at where he's taking me. One quick turn in the hallway, and I find myself in his bedroom. His walls are dark blue. There is a computer on his desk, some sports posters on the wall, a beanbag chair, and a double bed. When he closes the door behind us, I notice it has a lock. Suddenly, our candy date doesn't seem so innocent.

"Why the lock?" I ask.

"How else do you keep your parents out?"

When he puts it that way, it makes sense. But I'm pretty sure my parents wouldn't allow it. He disappears into his walk-in closet. When he returns, a snake is dangling from his hand. I watch as its muscles tighten and its body begins to curl around his arm.

"This is Diablo," he says. "He's a ball python — almost a metre long."

He walks toward me, holding the snake out. I put my hand up like a stop sign. "I don't like snakes."

As if seeing a meal, the snake lifts his head, flicking its forked tongue at me. Just watching it makes my skin crawl. I start backing up.

Holding the head still, Colter extends the body toward me. "Just touch his back. His skin feels really cool."

"Get it away or I'm leaving."

"Party-pooper," he says, putting the snake back in its cage. "You need to trust me. I know Diablo. He would never hurt you . . . unless you hurt him first. Then you couldn't really blame him, could you?"

"Uhh ... I guess not."

Walking over to his laptop, he says, "Come see the YouTube videos I found yesterday."

The videos are hilarious, and after a few minutes, I start to relax and forget about the snake. Colter puts on some tunes and I sit on the carpet.

"I've been meaning to ask . . . what's Mel short for?"

I lean back on my hands and groan. "You don't want to know."

He comes and sits next to me. "Melanie?"

"I wish. That would be sweet."

"Melissa?"

"Nope."

He raps his knuckles on my head: "Melon?"

"What? Nooo!"

He must have shifted closer cuz suddenly our shoulders are touching. "How bad can it be?"

"Okay, you win, but don't let it get around. Melody," I say, my voice deflating.

I expect him to laugh, but he doesn't. "That's a nice name," he says.

I can't believe I'm opening up to him like this . . . already. "My mom plays the cello," I explain. "When I was born, she had this crazy idea that if she named me Melody, I would grow to love music as much as she does."

"And?"

"I take Fine Arts."

He grins. "You're a rebel." Leaning back on his elbows, he stares at the ceiling. "What's the story with you and Dustin? You seem close — more than friends."

"Nope. He's got a girlfriend, and they're tight." Right now, Dustin is the last person I want to think about, so I change the subject. "Where are you from?" I ask, playing innocent.

"I transferred from Ryder — couldn't get the course I needed."

"So . . ." I say, narrowing my eyes at him. "Why'd you let me go on and on about Sarnia yesterday?"

He gives me a sheepish grin. "You were so enthusiastic . . . I liked listening to you talk. I was gonna say something, but then your pal Dustin walked in." He goes quiet and just stares at me, and I can feel the mood in the room changing. "Your eyes . . ." he whispers, "they're ocean blue."

At first, I look away, feeling uncomfortable. But I can't help wondering where all this is heading. I find myself returning his stare. "The flecks of gold in your eyes look like flames."

"Water and fire: an interesting combination," he says. "Fire can hurt you."

"True . . ." I say, rising to the challenge. "But water puts out fire. Therefore, I must have power over you."

"I believe that," he says, his voice going husky. "Ever since we met, I've been thinking about you."

He looks deep into my eyes, and I'm melting in his heat. His hand brushes the side of my leg as he leans in closer. Thinking he's going to kiss me, I part my lips, waiting. Without warning, he rolls away. I'm not sure if he's teasing me or has re-considered the kiss. I'm relieved and, at the same time, disappointed. Things are moving a bit too fast.

"Let's eat the almond bark," he says, getting up.

Between the fuzzy peaches and the almond bark, I'm on a sugar high when he drops me at the apartment. He kisses me — not more than a peck, but it does not disappoint. He's letting me know he's interested, but moving slowly. The tension between us is delicious.

Chapter 7

Follow your heart: it's the path to true love. But what if your heart doesn't know the difference between love and obsession? Everyone knows the heart is just an organ — and that thoughts and emotions come from the brain. And we all know there are a lot of defective brains out there.

For a long time, my brain has been telling me that Dustin is the one. Even though he's dating Gina, I secretly thought he felt the same way about me. I saw it in little things — like the special way he looked at me, and how he walked a little closer to me than to others, and how he confided in me, told me stuff he would never trust with Gina. Or . . . did I just want to believe it? After all, no one forced him to go out with her. Uggg . . . frrrrustrating. Stop thinking about him!

In the morning, Peyton and I pass Dustin and Gina in the hall. She's leaning on her locker, her arms gripped around his waist.

"Not cool at school," Peyton comments as we walk by.

"Shhh!" I warn. "They'll hear."

"That's the point," she says, hitting me with her backpack.

"Change the subject," I insist.

"Fine, there's something I wanted to tell you. After you dropped me off, I went on Colter's Facebook. His old girlfriend: did you notice anything odd?"

"No. What?"

"Duh . . . she could be your twin. You both have long hair with side bangs, and you have the same blue eyes."

"She's way prettier," I insist.

"No, she's not. She just likes to pose for the camera. It's strange, that's all. You should ask him about her."

"I will . . . when the time is right. It's not exactly cool to talk about old girlfriends when you first meet a guy."

There are ten minutes before the bell rings, so Peyton and I grab a couple of green teas and sit down in the cafeteria. Green tea is part of the school's new healthy menu, along with fresh salads and tofu burgers.

"Tell me what happened yesterday," she says, her eyes twinkling.

"I texted you about everything," I remind her.

She leans in close. "You were short on details.

Start with the part where you thought he was going to kiss you." Peyton is impressed with the new action in my life. She's determined to squeeze out every last juicy detail of my first date. And I admit, I am having fun telling her.

At lunch, I'm choking down a dry almond butter sandwich. Glancing around the cafeteria, I can't find Colter. Dustin is sitting with his buddies from the reserve. He gets up and walks over, scowling.

"What's got you in a foul mood?" I joke. "Chicken for lunch?"

He doesn't laugh. "Is it true? You don't want to be around me?"

"I — uh — who told you that?"

"Message received," he says, storming out of the cafeteria.

I glare across the table at Peyton. "How could you? That was private, between us."

"Don't look at me," she says, shaking her head. "I didn't say anything. Maybe someone overheard us: Gina?"

I slump down in my chair. "Dustin hates me now."

"He doesn't hate you. He's just mad. It'll blow over."

"Maybe . . ." I say, but I'm not so sure.

My cell goes off. It's Colter.

"sit with me in art"

"ya sure. where r u?"

"home"

"ok. see u later"

When it's fourth period, I sit on the stool next to Colter. Dustin doesn't notice since he's slouched forward over his work. When he finally looks up, I don't see his grumpy reaction because I look away.

One hollow eye is staring up from Colter's sketchbook. He's busy drawing the corner of a second eye. His charcoal pencil is making delicate, feathery strokes.

"Just eyes?" I say. "No face to go with them?"

He shakes his mop of hair. "The eyes are the window to the soul."

"You've drawn two black pits."

He makes an evil face. "I'm just giving the teacher what he wants, something dark and disturbing. Where's your assignment?"

"On the racks. I drew circles."

He gives me one of his dimply grins. "Nice."

I set up my palette, determined to actually paint something today. But Colter and I are goofing around and having too much fun to take art therapy seriously. In any other class, we wouldn't get away with this. But Mr. Passingham has a high tolerance for classroom disorder. Since he has ADHD, he understands what it's like to feel restless in class. He allows students to walk around the room and talk, as long as they don't disrupt the others.

Eventually, I decide on shades of grey and blue and start drawing waves in an ocean. Soon I get inspired to include a leaping dolphin.

Colter makes fun of my picture. "There is no emotion, not a drop."

"Happy emotion," I insist. "What's wrong with that?"

"The only thing deep is the water."

"You asked for it!" I load up my brush and dab some blue on his nose.

Unfortunately, I go too far and attract Mr. Passingham's attention. "Guido!" he calls to me. "Keep your creative strokes on the canvas." He's referring to Guido Daniele, the famous Italian body painter.

The class chuckles — everyone, that is, except Dustin, who gives me a hard stare.

When Colter leaves to wash his face at the sink, I concentrate on my painting. I don't care what anyone else thinks: the dolphin makes me happy. I can't say the same about circles.

Chapter 8

After school, I'm grabbing my running shoes and shorts from my locker when Colter walks up. I'm in a hurry, so I can't linger.

"Wanna go to DQ?" he asks. "I'll pay."

"I've got volleyball tryouts," I tell him.

"You'd rather play volleyball than hang out with me?"

"Umm . . ." I'm not sure if he's being serious.

"I've got an idea," he says. "I'll work out in the weight room and we'll go after."

"Sweet!"

Volleyball is the one sport I'm good at. I'm not a natural athlete, but I've worked hard at developing as a player. I started playing in grade seven at my elementary school in Calgary. Every year, I play in a beach volleyball league. If I slack off, someone else will be ready to take my spot on the school team.

Colter and I walk off in different directions. I head to the locker room to get changed. A few minutes later, I find him wandering the halls, lost. Meridian High is supposed to be a "student-friendly" school. The main section houses the offices, two gyms, and the cafeteria. The classrooms are located down six separate wings. Sending students down these long, narrow halls is supposed to be safer and less crowded. The result is a bunch of confused students. During September, it's easy to pick out the grade nines. They're hopelessly lost.

At most schools, the weight room is near the gym. At Meridian High, you go past Gym A and then enter Wing 4, where the weight room is located behind classroom 4C. I try to explain this to Colter but realize it's easier to take him. By the time I arrive at tryouts, the others are already running in the halls.

Coach Burns walks up to me. She is short, muscular, and overly serious. "Mel Rankin," she says, clipboard in hand, "you were on the team last year. What do I expect?"

"Commitment," I respond automatically. She's drilled this into our heads.

She puts a mark beside my name and says, "Don't be late again."

I try to explain that I was helping a new student, but she doesn't care. Sucks! I don't want to get on Coach's wrong side before the team's even picked. Sprinting off down the hall, I spot Peyton ahead. She's slacking off, so I easily catch up.

"It's over," she moans when I fall in step beside her. "Chad and I broke up."

"Oh, Peyton, I'm so sorry. What happened?"

"I told him his 'doughnut' excuse was lame. We got into a huge argument over Rachael. I said some stupid things, and then he just walked away. *He* broke up with *me!*"

"Don't worry," I say, trying to reassure her. "He'll cool down. You two are great together."

"No. You didn't see him." She lets out a long suffering sigh. "Maybe it's for the best."

I can tell by the look on her face she doesn't feel that way.

By the time I finish my laps, the others are lining up for drills. Before Coach lets me join them, she makes me complete three sets of finger-tip push-ups on the wall to warm up my hands. We're practising serves — my strength. When it's my turn, I take my stance, concentrate, and toss the ball up. Wham! I slam it into the net. Next time up, I catch the top of the net. I'm not worried. A little practice and I'll have my serve right where I want it — clearing the top of the net by a bee's breath.

I'm leaving the gym after practice when I see the little guy from the fight the other day. He's got a nasty shiner in shades of purple and yellow. There's a blood spot in the corner of one eye that looks like red jelly. A line of stitches is visible through his left eyebrow.

I walk up to him and smile. "How's it going?"

My legs go weak as I watch the jelly pulsing in his eye.

"I feel better than I look," he says. "The headaches are gone."

"Is that Joe dude leaving you alone?"

"Yeah, your friend saved my ass. I owe him."

"He was happy to help," I say. "But if I were you, I'd stay away from Joe's girlfriend."

"You saw Joe Simmons," he says. "Do I look stupid?" He holds up one hand. "Don't answer that. His girlfriend, Ashanti, is in my Math class. The other day, she failed a major test and was considering dropping the class. Lori wants to be a nurse and she needs to pass Math, so I offered to tutor her. That's when she kissed me on the cheek. Joe was walking down the hall and saw. He lost it . . . started threatening me with his fist, warning, 'Touch my girl and pay the price.' Ashanti got him to cool down, and I thought it was over."

"Joe sounds psycho," I say.

"Yeah, I don't know what Lori sees in him."

We talk until I notice Colter approaching. "Got to go," I say with a little wave. "See you around."

"Who was that?" Colter asks as we head to my locker.

"One of the guys from the fight."

"Wha'd he do to deserve that eye?"

"Nothing."

Colter gives a little laugh. "It's never 'nothing.'"

"The guy thought he made a move on his girlfriend," I explain.

"Then he deserved it."

"No, he didn't. He was trying to help her. They're friends."

"Ask any guy. They aren't looking for friend-ship."

"Oh, come on . . . lots of guys and girls are friends."

"Not in my world."

I corner him at my locker. "Oh, yeah, how is it in your world?"

"Let's see," he says, grinning. "It's me and you at DQ."

"Mmmm . . . I like the way you think," I say, grabbing my coat. "Let's go."

Chapter 9

The next few weeks are crazy. Colter calls me to do stuff all the time. One morning he texted me, "Grab your board . . . there's fresh snow."

We drove to Boler Mountain in London, Ontario, and boarded for six hours. The hills aren't big, but I loved feeling the snow under me again. The next day, Sarah and I were at Peyton's for a girls' night. We were making tacos for dinner when Colter showed up at her door with tickets to a Red Wings game in Detroit. I'm not into hockey, but he told me the tickets cost him a hundred bucks each. I didn't want to let him down. So I went, and we had a great time, even though I ditched my friends. They were pissed at me and didn't invite me to the movies the next night. Whatever . . . I had other plans anyway.

After being stuck at Aunt Stella's without a car for all these months, it feels amazing to be able to escape at a moment's notice. We've gone tobogganing, hiking, to the movies — we've even studied together. The only night I didn't see him was the time he and his dad were drinking together in his basement. Colter called it "bonding time." Wow! That's not what my parents consider bonding..

The only person I've been hanging with lately is Colter. I didn't plan it like this, and I'm not even sure how it happened. My life is in a whirl. All I know is this: I'm falling hard and fast for him.

After Peyton worked so hard to get us together, she's acting weird. She hasn't said anything specific, but I pick up a vibe when she's around Colter. I don't think she likes him. Like the other day, she said, "We'll go out for pizza after volleyball, if that's okay with Colter." Her snotty remark did not go unnoticed. Not only that, all of a sudden she's rooting for Dustin. She says I hurt him, and I should make it up to him. News flash! Dustin isn't the only one who got hurt. You can't lose someone special and not feel pain. Just this morning, I passed him in the hall. He was walking with his little buddy, Ben. He walked past me like I was invisible. Ouch.

I'm at the apartment, making a grilled cheese sandwich for dinner, when my cell goes off. It's Peyton.

"My parents are going to a wedding," she announces. "They're leaving Saturday morning. It's a six-hour drive. Best news: THEY'RE STAYING OVERNIGHT!"

"Party!" I cry. "I'll bring Colter. It'll give him a chance to get to know some of the guys."

"Sure."

Was it my imagination, or did her voice drop?

"Are you inviting Chad?" Peyton and Chad were still officially broken up, but it wasn't exactly over.

"Maybe . . . if I see him around."

She acts like she doesn't care, but she can't fool me.

When I arrive at school on Thursday morning, I find a note in my locker:

Meet me after school.

C

Colter must have forgotten that today is the final volleyball tryout. My serve is finally under control and I'm pumped to start the season. I don't see him until last period, and then I corner him. "How did you get in my locker?" I ask.

He flips open my art portfolio to the back cover. That's where I wrote down my combination, along with Peyton's and Dustin's. "You should have asked first," I tell him.

Ignoring my comment, he says, "Is it a date?"

"I have volleyball, remember?"

He grabs a pen and writes "Skip it" on my arm below my elbow.

"No, it's the last night of tryouts."

"Aw, come on, you're a shoo-in. It's important or I wouldn't ask."

I shake my head. "What's so frikkin' important?"

He leans over and whispers in my ear. "It's a secret."

I admit: I am curious.

"What's your aunt's last name?" he asks, pen in hand.

"Taylor. Why?"

Tearing a page from his binder, he writes:

Attention: Coach Burns,

Please excuse Melody Rankin from volleyball tryouts, as she has an urgent doctor's appointment.

Stella Taylor, Guardian

"Urgent?" I say, cracking up. "You make it sound like I'm dying. Seriously, I'm not —"

Mr. Passingham interrupts us. "Mel, your paint is drying on the palette. Perhaps you could dip your brush once in a while."

I get down to work, but Colter doesn't let up, and by the bell, he's worn me down. We head to the gym to find Coach Burns. While we're waiting, my stomach starts doing flips. "I don't want to do this. I'm a terrible liar."

"Just hand it to her," he insists. "You don't have to say anything."

"But she'll see the guilty look on my face."

We clam up when Coach walks out of the equipment room, carrying the volleyball net and the bag of balls.

Colter squeezes my hand. "Don't chicken out."

Nervously walking over, I hand her the note. "I — uh — this is for you."

She reads it, then looks up at me. "What's wrong with you?"

A question like that can be taken two ways. "It's p-personal," I stammer. "But it won't affect my game."

"Are you sure?"

I nod mutely.

"Alright," she says slowly.

As we're walking away, I grab Colter's arm. "This had better be good."

In the car, Colter still won't tell me where we're going. We've been on so many adventures, anything is possible. "A clue," I beg.

He shakes his head and smiles. Then he cranks up the tunes and accelerates. We cruise through downtown and head south, past Chemical Valley with the massive petrochemical industries. Travelling along the river road, he finally pulls into a spot at the edge of the water. The St. Clair River is frozen, a solid mass of ice and snow clear across to Michigan. A coyote is picking its way along the ice — poor thing looks starving.

Colter hasn't said a word and I'm starting to get pissed, thinking: *I cut practice for this?* I regard him with a withering stare. "Is *this* the surprise?"

Running his fingers through my hair, he says, "I spent a long time picking the perfect spot."

I'm about to say something nasty when he reaches past me into the glove compartment and brings out a small box. "Open it."

"What is it?" I ask, my eyes widening.

"You'll see."

I remove the white bow, lift the top, and find myself staring at a diamond ring. It's not a chip — it's an actual stone. It doesn't look like a promise ring; it looks like an engagement ring. The stone glitters like genuine rays of sunshine . . . but at what cost? I'm sixteen — not ready for a big commitment.

He leans over and kisses me. "I think about you all the time. I want us to be together always."

"Huh?" I say, stunned.

"Will you be my girlfriend?"

"Ohhh . . ." I let out a gush of air. I thought I *was* his girlfriend. For one crazy moment, I thought he was going to propose. "You didn't have to get me an expensive ring."

He looks hurt. "Don't you like it?"

"It's not that . . . it's beautiful."

"So are you," he says, kissing me again. "I love you."

He loves me? We've only been together a few weeks! He slips the ring on my right ring finger. A perfect fit. I turn my hand on different angles to catch the sparkle. While I'm distracted, he flips open his cell and holds it up to the windshield. "Ready?" He tips his head next to mine. "Smile. I'll put this on my Facebook."

He shows me the picture. Ughhh . . . I've got that "deer in the headlights" look. When he snapped the picture, I was suddenly reminded of Jillian, his old girlfriend. Was he this way with her?

"I have to confess something," I blurt. "When we met, I went on your Facebook. You had a girlfriend . . . and it was obvious you were serious. And now us . . . so fast. I don't want to pry but —"

He turns to me with a blank look. "She's no threat to you."

"But . . . how can you —"

"Stop!" I can tell something's wrong by the look on his face. Even so, I'm not prepared for what comes next. Looking away, he drops his voice. "She's dead."

Stunned, I shut my mouth.

"It was an accident." He drops his head on the steering wheel. "I can't talk about it . . . not now."

There is so much pain in his voice. Oh, boy, I've really messed up. The guy is giving me a ring, expressing his feelings, and I corner him about his old girlfriend — who, as it turns out, is dead.

"I'm sorry for bringing it up," I say. "This was not the right time. I'm such an idiot."

"No," he says, putting his arm around me. "You are perfect. You didn't know." We stare out over the ice, and I'm trying hard to think of something cheerful to talk about.

"Peyton's having a party on Friday night," I say, raising my voice enthusiastically. "We're invited."

"Oh." His voice drops. "Who's going to be there?"

"I don't know . . . everyone, probably, since her parents are away. You could bring a couple of friends from Ryder. Peyton wouldn't mind."

He pulls his arm away and stares ahead.

"What's wrong?" I ask.

"I wanted be alone with you on Friday night."

"Peyton will be pissed if I don't go," I explain. "Besides, it'll be fun."

"Peyton is annoying."

I fold my arms. "She's my best friend."

He's upset, drumming his fingers on the steering wheel. But then, just as quickly, he lets it go. "Today is about us," he says, pulling me close.

His lips meet mine and lock in a delicious, wet kiss. Nothing else matters.

Chapter 10

Friday morning I catch up with Peyton in the school parking lot.

"I dreamed about you last night," she says, cracking up. "You showed up at a rock concert wearing a sparkling prom dress. Your hair was in a fancy up-do."

"What was I thinking?" I cry. "How embarrassing!"

The temperature is above zero, so we linger outside the school, talking. "You're coming tonight, right?" she asks, like it's not even a question.

"Ummm . . . I'm not sure."

Her head snaps back as if I slapped her. "You have to come . . . and stay over, like always."

"I know, but . . ." I hold out my right hand. "Colter gave me this yesterday."

She grabs my finger and examines the ring up

close. "Whoa, nice bling! Chad gave me a bracelet made of pennies."

"You love that bracelet!" I remind her.

She flips her hair back and smiles. "Yeah, you're right."

The front entrance is getting crowded, so I lower my voice. "He used the L word."

"Lust?" she says, giving me a hard time.

I knock her with my elbow. "No . . . you know."

"Already? But you hardly know each other." She steps back and studies my face. "Did you say it back?"

"I couldn't," I admit. "Not yet. Love is a big deal, and I am still getting over Dustin."

I can actually hear her sigh of relief.

"About Friday," I say, fumbling for the right words. "It's our first real date. Colter wants to be alone — maybe do dinner and a movie."

She rolls her eyes. "No offence, Mel, but you two have been alone 24/7 already."

"We've been hanging, mostly," I try to explain. "Studying together . . . stuff like that."

"The only thing you've been studying is each other." She bites her lower lip. "You've been spending *all* your time with him. And you keep ditching me and Sarah. What gives?"

"I'm sorry," I tell her. "It's just that Colter needs someone in his life right now. His parents are messed up, and . . . I just found out his girlfriend died in an accident."

"Ohhh! That's awful. What kind of accident?"

"He was too upset to talk about it. But I am going to find out."

"Yeah, I'd want to know. Anyway . . . about the party —"

"Don't worry," I reassure her. "I'm not going to let any guy come between us. I'll be at the party."

"Yes!" She hugs me. "We're going to have sooo much fun!"

***

I'm dressed in skinny jeans and a silky pink top. Colter looks hot in his collared shirt with rolled-up sleeves. Before we leave for the party, he snaps a couple of pictures to mark our first "official" date. Even though this is not the night he imagined, he's being cool about it.

We arrive at Peyton's shortly after eight. The place is already crowded and Drake is pounding out of the speakers. Peyton waves from across the room, then rushes over, her wild berry scent following her.

"Love your top!" I yell over the music.

"Thanks," she says. "Do you think the red is too . . . screaming? Does it clash with my hair?"

"It's perfect," I tell her.

She turns to Colter and says, "Mind if I steal Mel? I need help with a recipe."

"No problem," he replies, but I detect metal in his voice.

"I won't be long," I promise. As we're heading

to the kitchen, I turn to her. "Recipe? Since when do you cook?"

"That's where you come in. I want to make punch."

"How about blender drinks," I suggest. "Everyone loves them."

She shakes her head. "I'm hiding the blender. Chad broke it at the last party when he got the bright idea to invent a healthy drink."

"Oh, yeah," I recall, laughing. "Real healthy! He was trying to blend carrots and celery with vodka . . . called it the Veg-Out."

In the fridge, I find a couple of bottles of Sprite and some orange juice. The only fruit is lemon and kiwi. "This might be weird," I say, making a face. "But let's see what happens." We throw it all together and agree the floating circles of lemon and kiwi look kind of exotic.

"Do you think we've made enough?"

"Depends," I say thoughtfully. "Are you spiking it?"

"Nope. This is for the designated drivers. No one ever makes them a special drink."

"Then it'll last."

My eyes wander to the other room, hoping to catch a glimpse of Dustin. We used to have fun together at parties. Now that we're both in relationships and I've stopped chasing after him, I don't see why we can't be friends again. Peyton certainly thinks so. This party is my chance to make things right . . . if only he'd show. But I don't see him — or Colter, for that matter.

"I should go find Colter," I tell Peyton. "He doesn't really know anyone."

"You don't have to babysit him," she insists. She fills a red plastic cup with punch and hands it to me. "Taste test."

"Sweet and tangy," I say, smacking my lips together.

"Just like us," she says, grinning.

With my hands, I form a halo over my head. "I'm the sweet one."

"Not so sure about that!" she says, laughing. "Your life is crazier than mine these days."

"Crazier than you and Chad? Not even close!"

When Peyton's cell rings, I leave the kitchen to check on Colter. I find him talking to Buzz and Jeff, a couple of guys from the football team. Also, I notice he's holding a beer. Suddenly, the night is complicated. Colter brought his car and we're supposed to be going to the late movie, which begins in forty minutes. When I told Peyton we were coming to her party, I actually meant dropping by. It was the only way I could get Colter to agree.

Heading back to the kitchen, I clink plastic cups with Peyton. "Cheers! I'm the DD."

Peyton and I are joking around when a couple of guys we've never seen before walk up. One is wearing a green ball cap, and he's got long sideburns. The other is wearing a Ryder T-shirt.

The guy in the ball cap leans on the kitchen counter. "Wha'cha got to drink?"

Peyton glares at him. "You're drunk, and you weren't invited . . . so leave."

"You Meridian girls think you're too good for us?"

"Seriously, my parents —"

"What parents? I don't see any." He turns to his buddy. "You see Ma and Pa?"

He shakes his head. "I don't think she's telling the truth."

The one in the Ryder T-shirt waggles his tongue at me. "You're cute. Wanna get friendly?" He puts his arm around my waist.

"Get off me!" I snarl, jerking away.

Grabbing a cup, he drags it and his fingers through the punch. He tastes it, then spits it in the sink. "This tastes like shit."

"You should know. You're full of it!" I fire back.

The situation is getting out of control. Peyton disappears and quickly returns with six football players. As the Ryder guys are being escorted out, I hear one of them yell, "Hey, Wagner, any accidents lately?"

"Piss off," Colter yells back, then he storms into the kitchen and slams his fist on the counter. "Why were you talking to those guys?"

"Who were they?" I ask. "And what did they mean by 'accident'? Did it have something to do with Jillian?"

He gives me a cold stare. "They're losers from my old school. I don't want you associating with those types."

"Whoa!" I say. "You really need to chill. I can take care of myself." Seeing how upset he is, I drop the subject for now. "I saw you talking to Buzz," I say.

"Yeah, he's cool. He told me Meridian's football team needs a strong receiver. That's the position I play."

As if on cue, Buzz walks up and hands Colter another beer. I smile to myself, realizing we're not going to make the movie. Buzz is keeping Colter supplied with beer and he looks happy, so I bounce off to talk to my girlfriends. When Chad and Dustin arrive, I get the feeling the night is going to get interesting. Peyton and Chad may have broken up, but the way they look at each other, its soooo not over. But right now, I'm concentrating on Dustin, wondering why he's not with Gina. When he looks my way, I give him a little wave, and before I know it, I'm walking over to him.

"Hey. Can we talk?"

Chad gets the message and leaves.

"What's up?" Dustin says, looking right past me.

He's trying to hide his feelings, but I can tell he is hurt. If he knew the real reason I chose to stay away . . . if the truth wasn't so hard . . .

Somehow, I've got to make things right. The party room is too loud for a serious conversation, so we head to the living room. I wish I had planned this moment. As it is, I have no idea what to say. He leans against the wall, waiting for me to speak.

Meanwhile, I'm fumbling in my head for something he'll believe . . . that isn't the pathetic truth. It doesn't help that I'm a lousy liar, especially around people I care about. Opening my mouth, I try to wing it: "I thought I should stay away from you cuz — uh — Gina doesn't like me . . . and, well, the feeling's mutual, but —"

He cuts me off. "This is not about Gina."

"Huh?"

"Colter told me you didn't want to hang out with anyone from the reserve."

"What?" I stand there, stunned. "I never said that! Why would Colter say such a rotten thing?"

He shrugs, and I'm not sure he believes me.

"Dustin, you know I don't feel that way. Why would you listen to him?"

He takes a step toward me, searching for the truth in my eyes. "Last year, when you wouldn't go out with me, after you told me you liked me . . . I asked if it was because I'm from the reserve."

"Yeah, and if you remember correctly, I clearly told you that wasn't it. I said I didn't want to hurt Travis."

"That's what you said, but then you turned around and dumped him."

I throw my arms up in frustration. "Cuz he cheated on me!"

"Oh . . ." His voice drops. "You never told me."

"Well, I didn't exactly feel great about the whole thing." Tears start rolling down my cheeks. "Honestly, sometimes you are so clueless!"

The look in his eyes softens and he gathers me in his arms. I linger, enjoying the familiar warmth. "I've missed you," I confess.

Without warning, a rough hand slams across my back. "Slut!" Violently, I'm thrown face-first into the wall. Hitting hard, I crumple to my knees. It took one second for my whole world to explode.

Chapter 11

I get up off the floor, feeling dizzy and disoriented. When my head starts to clear, I start to process what's happening.

"Don't you ever touch her!" Colter's voice is low and menacing. He's somehow managed to pin Dustin to the wall. A curious crowd is gathering.

"Get your hands off me!" Dustin warns, straining to break free. Colter leans in, pressing his forearm hard into Dustin's chest in the spot right below his throat. Colter doesn't know who he's dealing with. Dustin is undefeated in his wrestling division, and he never stays pinned for long. In an explosive move, he arches his back and sends Colter hurling backward onto the floor. Dustin pounces on him, like an animal after prey. The floor is Dustin's turf. He's spent years perfecting his moves. The school drills a "code of conduct" into their wrestlers: anyone who intentionally hurts another person is off the team. Something tells me the code doesn't apply tonight.

Dustin slams Colter hard, just once, and I hear the air burst from his lungs. Rolling on the ground, he gasps and clutches his chest. The colour drains from his face.

I rush over to Dustin and cry, "What have you done?"

"Knocked the wind out of him," he says, looking pleased with himself. "He'll be okay in a minute."

The way Colter's heaving for breath, it sounds like he's dying. But Buzz is helping him, and I stick around, watching from a distance. When he starts breathing normally, I walk away with Dustin. "I don't know what got into him. I've never seen him like this."

"I don't care about him!" he snaps. "Are you okay? You fell."

Obviously, Dustin didn't see everything. *Probably best to keep it that way,* I tell myself. *Things are bad enough.*

"I'm fine," I insist, even as I feel the side of my face swelling.

From a distance, I've been keeping an eye on Colter. He's standing up now and walking across the room. When I take a step toward him, Dustin grabs me. "Don't," he says.

"I have to," I insist. "He can't go around attacking people!"

"Whatever. Go, then." He's pissed, and I don't blame him after everything.

As I approach Colter, we exchange angry glares. "What's wrong with you?" I snarl through my teeth.

He points an accusing finger at me. "Shut up before I —"

"Before you what?"

Peyton appears and starts pulling me away. "He can't talk to you like that."

"Get back here!" he orders. "We're not done!"

"Yes, we are!"

Peyton and I head to the washroom and lock the door. "What's going on?" she asks. "I was in my bedroom talking to my parents. They had phoned to say they arrived safely. When I came downstairs, Chad said Colter and Dustin had been going at it."

"We hugged," I say, my voice starting to break. "That's all. Colter saw and he completely lost it."

Sitting on the toilet, I slump forward and dissolve into tears. Peyton is stroking my hair and giving me advice. I don't know what I'd do without her. For all the drama she's put me through with her boyfriends, she's giving it back to me in spades.

My cell rings. It's Colter. I don't answer.

He texts me. "I love u. dont shut me out."

I switch off my phone and shove it in my pocket. With barely room for a sink and a toilet, the washroom feels like it's closing in on me. Peyton and I make a plan to sneak up to her bedroom. We take a couple of steps out the door, and suddenly he's there, grabbing my arm.

"Talk to me. Come on, baby, you know I'd never hurt you."

Peyton steps between us. "You'd better leave."

Ignoring her, he begs, "Give me a chance to explain. That's all I'm asking."

His anger is gone, and I need answers, so I finally agree. Peyton doesn't want to leave us alone, but I promise her I'll be fine. We sit across from each other in the living room, and I fix my eyes on the oriental carpet, waiting for him to speak.

"The way he was holding you — I thought he was coming on to you." He sounds tired, defeated.

Gripping the arms of the chair, I shake my head. "You called me a slut."

"Come on," he says. "It was the booze talking — the words just slopped out of my mouth. You know I don't feel that way."

I answer him with a glare. "Did the alcohol make you throw me into the wall, too?"

"I'd never hurt you. I was going after him." When I don't say anything, he tosses his hands up. "I didn't even throw a punch. Hey, I'm a guy. We tend to go a little insane when we think someone is hitting on our girlfriends!"

"Okay," I say, determined to stay strong. "Then tell me this. Why did you shovel that load of crap to Dustin . . . telling him I didn't want to be friends? Are you that threatened by him?"

He lets out a long sigh. "It wasn't my idea. Gina begged me to do it. She thought she was losing Dustin."

"You and Gina teaming up." I give a pathetic laugh. "That's just great."

Who is this guy? Part of me wants to tell him to screw off and end this relationship right now. But just a few hours ago, I was caught up in a whirlwind romance, and I was happy. Should I give it all up for the sake of one bad night? Colter had a serious meltdown. Was it a one-time thing? Or is there something deeper, a crack running straight to his core? I can't think about it anymore, so I tell him I need some space and ask him to leave.

"Fine," he says, slowly nodding, "but I probably shouldn't drive."

"Call a taxi," I say.

"It's just a couple of miles. I can make it."

"Are you serious? Do you want to lose your licence?" Frustrated, I hold out my hand. "Give me the stupid keys. I'll drive you home."

We grab our coats and leave quietly so I don't have to deal with either Peyton or Dustin.

"You can drop me off and keep the car tonight," he says. "I'll get it tomorrow."

We drive to his place in silence. Before he gets out, he tries to kiss me, but I pull away. "Aw, come on, it was our first fight," he says. "Don't we get to make out . . . I mean, make up?"

"You're acting drunk," I say, pushing him away.

"Sober as a church mouse," he says, grinning.

"What are you talking about?"

"I have no idea," he says, reaching for the door handle. "But I'll see you tomorrow."

After I drop Colter off, I head straight to the apartment. As soon as I walk in, I smell Aunt Stella's musky perfume and realize she's home. Even though we rarely talk about anything important, she has a ton of experience with relationships — most of them bad. Maybe she can help me understand what happened tonight.

"Hey," I say, giving her a little wave.

"You're home early," she calls from the living room. "Did you have fun?"

"No. Can we talk?"

"I'd love to. Unfortunately, now is not a good time."

That's when I notice two wine glasses on the coffee table. A man walks out of the washroom. "This is Mark," she says, giving me a little wink.

"Hey," I say, not trying to hide my disappointment. Then I head straight to my bedroom.

"We'll talk later," she calls after me.

No we won't, I'm thinking. *You won't even remember.*

Lying on my bed, I text Peyton to let her know I'm okay. She's bummed I'm not staying over, but understands that I want to be in my own bed tonight. Suddenly, I get a strong urge to dial long distance. Mom answers. An aching knot forms in my throat.

"Hey."

"Mel!" she cries, alarmed. "Is everything alright?"

"Yeah . . . I just miss you."

Chapter 12

It's easy to get up early when you don't go to sleep. First thing in the morning, I drive to Peyton's to help her clean up the house. She greets me in pyjama pants, holding a toilet brush. Her red hair is tangled and mascara is smudged under her eyes.

"Buzz puked in the bathroom," she says, looking like she might do the same. "He missed the toilet and it seeped under the baseboards. What should I do?"

"Can't help," I tell her. "I don't do bathrooms."

"But it smells really bad."

"Call Buzz," I suggest. "Make him clean up his own mess."

"Yeah, right, like that would ever happen." Swinging the toilet brush, she corners me by the front door. "About last night . . ."

"Get that thing away from me," I insist, pushing her arm.

"Are you breaking up with him?"

"We'll talk later . . . I'm not awake yet. Besides, we should get cleaning before your parents walk in."

Leaving Peyton to deal with the bathroom, I start gathering beer bottles and plastic cups. My shoulder hurts, and my cheek is still red from where my face slapped the wall. It took careful blending with foundation to even out the tone. I'm lucky; it could have been so much worse.

An hour later, Peyton's place is looking good. We're sitting at the kitchen table drinking Coke and eating leftover chips. Peyton leans forward in her chair. "We've got to talk about last night. What are you going to do?"

I stare down at my Coke. "Dunno. I'm seeing him today to see if we can work it out . . . or not. When I got home last night, we talked online. He told me the court has ordered him to visit his mom in Florida, and that put him on edge at the party. He's leaving tomorrow for a week. He really doesn't want to see her — says he's never forgiven her for abandoning him." I pause. "There's something else. He told me he was going to take a couple of his dad's pills to chill out."

"What?" she says frowning. "That's messed up."

I bite my lip. "I don't think he's done that before . . . but I wouldn't know. And . . . yeah, I know it's not good."

The room goes silent. "Why did his mom leave?" she asks finally.

"Colter told me his parents were always fighting. His dad wouldn't let her work or even go to the grocery store alone. He screened her phone calls. But I don't know the whole story."

Peyton sighs. "I feel bad for Colter — honestly, I do, Mel — but that doesn't excuse his behaviour." She pauses. "After you left the party, I heard what really happened."

"It was just a push," I say. "An accident . . . I was in his way." I don't know why I'm defending him.

"Well, I'm glad he's leaving for a bit," she says. "You need some time to untangle your mind."

She's right. I can't think straight right now. Gazing out the window, I watch a woodpecker tap tap tap on a tree. Peyton clears her throat to get my attention. "Last night, when the Ryder guy made that comment about 'accidents' . . . did you ask Colter what he meant?"

I nod thoughtfully. "When we were online, I came right out and asked him about Jillian. I get the feeling she plays a part in all of this. He said he couldn't talk about it on the computer . . . that he'd tell me today."

"Good, cuz it bothered me all night."

I take a swig of pop and change the subject. "What happened between you and Chad last night?"

Peyton's mood brightens instantly. "We

connected at the party . . . just talked . . . but it's a start. Maybe I have been overreacting."

"Wow, Peyton, *you* overreact? I can't imagine."

We both laugh.

"Wanna go to the mall for smoothies?" she asks, getting up. "I owe you for helping me."

I hold up my Coke. "Dehydrated?"

She grins. "Like the desert."

"Can't," I say, pouting. "I have to return Colter's car — said I'd be there at eleven." I check my watch. "That's in twelve minutes."

Peyton doesn't look impressed, but she holds her tongue. "Let me know how it goes."

As I'm driving to his house, I brace myself for whatever is coming next. When Colter answers the door, I hold out his keys. "No dents."

"Phew!" he grins, wiping his brow. He's wearing cut-off sweats and a ripped T-shirt. His hair is tousled. Even when he doesn't try, he looks good. Pixie is hiding under the table as usual. When I try to coax her out, she pees on the white shag.

"Stupid mutt!" He grabs her by the collar and puts her outside.

"It's not her fault. I scared her."

"Everything scares Pixie. The only reason Dad keeps her is to punish my mother. She's the one who liked the dog."

"Well, then, you should convince your dad to do the right thing — send her to Florida."

"Not my problem," he says, walking away.

After I blot up the mess with paper towels, we

go to his bedroom, but only after he promises to leave his snake in the closet. He shows me some new YouTube videos. There's one of a dog hiding its bone in a basket of dirty laundry. Another of a guy on a motorcycle crashing through a pyramid of open tomato juice cans. And my favourite: the dolphin and the double kayak. A couple is quietly paddling along when a dolphin leaps over the kayak, right between them. The guy is excitedly paddling in the direction of the dolphin; the screaming woman is paddling in reverse. They end up going nowhere.

While Colter's searching for more videos, I go sit in his beanbag chair. He's acting as if nothing happened last night, and I'm getting annoyed. "You said we were going to talk," I say, finally. "That's the reason I came over."

He looks up from his computer. "I don't want to do all the talking. Tell me about your family."

"Uh . . . okayyy." I get the feeling he's stalling, but I go along. "My family's pretty boring. They've been in Fort McMurray for six months now. Mom loves her job, collecting soil and water samples and testing them in a lab. Dad likes the money he's making driving monster trucks at Suncor Energy. My sister made the junior basketball team, and she snowboards at Vista Ridge, the local hill. They've gone on two weekend ski trips, one to Marmot Basin in Jasper and the other to Lake Louise. I am so jealous!" I pause, trying to think of more. "Chevy is cute as ever. And . . . that's about it."

Colter lets out a sigh. "Your family sounds awesome."

"Yeah, I'm lucky." I never really thought much about it before, but my family *is* pretty great. Even though they are across the country, I know I can count on them if I'm in trouble. Without that kind of support, Colter must feel so alone.

Turning from his laptop, he stares down at his folded hands. "When I was little, my mom used to take me to the animal farm to feed the ducks, and when the geese would chase me, she'd scoop me up and hiss right back at them. She would spend weeks planning my birthday parties and invite the whole class, so no one would feel left out. She was *that* kind of mom. How could she leave me with him? I don't get it. So what if things weren't perfect." Keeping his eyes focused on his hands, he goes on. "When she got to Florida, she texted me, saying she needed time to think. Two weeks later, she filed for divorce. That was a year ago."

"Ouch." I say, grimacing. "That must have been hard."

"Not for her," he says. "Her new life is a permanent vacation. She lives in a little house on a canal where she rescues injured pelicans. The locals call her the Pelican Angel."

"She doesn't sound like a bad person," I say.

"Just a bad mother," he says, frowning. "She's seeing a psychiatrist . . . and now, after all this time, she says she's ready to see me. She needed a shrink to figure out that she should see her own son." He laughs, but there is no laughter in his eyes.

"Maybe you and your mom will work things out on your visit," I say, trying to stay positive.

"At least I'll get to hang out with the pelicans," he mutters. Turning back to his computer, he logs on to Facebook. "I posted some pictures. Wanna see?"

"Sure." I walk over and shift the laptop screen so I can get a better view. There's the picture Colter took when he gave me the ring, the two of us leaving for Peyton's party, me alone (or so I thought) brushing my hair.

Closing his laptop, he turns to me with a strange, unsettling look. "I need to tell you something, but I'm not sure how to say it."

"Just tell me," I insist, growing tired. *After everything . . . how bad can it be?*

"I killed my girlfriend."

Chapter 13

I want to run, but I'm cemented in place. I force myself to breathe. Murderers go to jail — they don't attend Meridian High.

"Why did you say that?" I ask, slowly edging backward. "If it's some sort of warped joke, it's not funny."

"I'm not trying to be funny," he says, taking a step toward me.

"Are you trying to scare me? . . . Cuz it's working." When he doesn't answer, I say, "That's it — I'm out of here."

As I turn to leave, he steps around me, blocking my way. "Stop! You asked what's wrong with my life, and I'm going to tell you."

"No. This is too much."

With his fingers, he sweeps my bangs off my face. His touch sends cold shivers down my spine. Backing away, I walk over to the bed and perch stiffly on the edge. "So, now that I'm your prisoner, you might as well tell me."

"You would have found out, sooner or later," he says, pacing the floor. "It was in the newspaper."

I look at him with a mix of horror and confusion. "If it was public information, why didn't you tell me?"

He turns and stares out the window. "I didn't know how. I-I couldn't find the words. We were so happy. I didn't want to ruin it."

"Killing your girlfriend," I say, my voice filled with venom. "Yeah, that could do it." Swallowing hard, I summon the courage to ask, "How?"

"We were in her car," he says, keeping his focus on the window. "It was late. She was driving us home from a party when her cell rang. It had fallen between the seats, so I dug down and grabbed it. She asked me to hand it to her, but I held it over my head and said, 'Come and get it!' I didn't think she would lunge after it . . . or that the car would spin out of control and hit a tree." He closes his eyes. "She was killed instantly."

I hug myself, feeling limp. I had heard about the accident — Mom had told me. I remember her preaching to me about cell phones and driving. But I didn't know the people involved, and for me, that had been the end of it. Until now.

"Were you hurt?"

"I wish. They took me to the hospital for observation and let me go a couple of hours later. The tree hit the driver's side . . . Jillian."

"It was an accident," I say firmly. "You didn't mean to —"

"If I hadn't been fooling around . . ." his voice trails off. "Last semester, at Ryder . . . the looks, the whispers . . . I was the guy responsible for the death of the most popular girl at the school. That's why I transferred."

Overwhelmed, I sit in silence. I can't imagine what something like that would do to a person.

"Are you going to leave me?" he asks quietly.

I shake my head. After everything he's been through, how could I walk away?

"I was afraid to tell you," he goes on. "Every-one I love leaves. I-I just need a break. With you in my life, I know I can get my act together." He takes my hand. "Let's start over fresh. I'll take you home now and pick you up at six for dinner."

I nod without thinking.

When he drops me off, I collapse on my bed. I told Colter I wouldn't leave him, but I'm not sure that's what I want. Colter needs someone who's there for him . . . he's been through so much. But am I that person?

If I decide to walk away, what will he do? That's the part that scares me.

***

He picks me up at six, wearing a grey dress shirt and black pants, smelling of cologne.

"You look amazing!" he says, his eyes widening at the sight of me.

I'm not feeling amazing, but I look pretty good, considering. My hair is smooth and silky, thanks to my straightener and a new high-gloss serum. I'm wearing eyeliner, mascara, and clear lip gloss — a lot of makeup for me. I've paired my silver top with hoop earrings and skinny, black jeans. Colter's dad gave him a gift certificate to a fancy French restaurant, Le Petite Maison, so we're going out in style.

When we arrive, we enter a small, dark room with only a few tables. Ours is the only one with a bouquet of fresh flowers. Colter is the kind of guy who would think of stuff like that. A piano is playing softly in the background.

A smiling waiter walks up to us. He has a round face with a cartoonish moustache. "Bonjour," he says, with a dramatic swing of his arm. "What would Mademoiselle like to drink?"

"Water, please," I say.

"Bonne. Always a good choice."

Despite everything, I find myself giggling at the way he's speaking half French and half English with a terrible accent. When he leaves to get our drinks, Colter and I argue over whether his moustache is real. The menu is puzzling, and it makes me regret dropping French. I choose *la salade verte* and *le poulet grille* because I recognize the words. Colter orders *escargot* and *le filet de saumon*.

When the escargot arrives, Colter pops one in his mouth. "Oh, man, these snails taste amazing cooked in garlic butter."

"What happened to their shells?" I say, jokingly. "Poor things are naked . . . and dead."

"Try one." He spears one of the limp blobs and holds it out to me.

"Get that away!" I say, pushing the fork. "I don't eat bugs."

"They're not bugs."

"What are they, then?"

"I have no idea, and I don't care, as long as they taste good."

My chicken dinner is served in a light cream sauce with carrots and yellow zucchini. It tastes better than anything I've eaten in a long time.

Somehow, we're having a good time. It's easy to have fun with Colter. He makes me forget about everything and live in the moment. There are no heavy conversations tonight. We chill and talk about stupid stuff. When he kisses me goodbye, he tells me that he loves me, and I tell him that I'll miss him when he's in Florida.

But my smile drops as I watch him drive away. I pull the ring off my finger. Who am I kidding? I can't do this anymore.

Chapter 14

Sunday afternoon, Peyton drives me to the reserve. I've got one week to do exactly what I choose — and I choose to see Dustin. We haven't spoken since the party. We've texted back and forth a bit, but it's not the same. It's cold out today, even for February. At least the sun is shining and the snow-lined roads are clear. During the drive, Peyton and I are discussing the Chad situation — deciding whether or not she should try and get back with him. It occurs to me that we always have the same conversation.

"He still insists he wanted a doughnut," she says. "I believe him, although I think Rachael wanted more."

"So what?" I insist. "There will always be Rachaels in the world. All that matters is he didn't give in to her."

A smile breaks onto her face. "You're right.

Chad loves apple fritters. I shouldn't hold that against him."

Finally, Peyton has her big breakthrough. Maybe now, we can talk about something else. My cell goes off . . . again. "Who's that?" she asks.

"Colter. He sent five texts from the airport this morning and I haven't replied."

She makes a face at the windshield. "Checking up on you?"

"Yep, but I'm not answering."

Peyton takes her eyes off the road long enough to give me a devilish grin. "Colter's plane wasn't even off the ground this morning when you phoned, begging me to drive you to the reserve. Admit it— you want Dustin."

"You are so off base," I insist. "I want Dustin as a friend. Honestly, Peyton, it's all I can handle right now."

"Yeah," she agrees.

We're driving past Chemical Valley. The area is huge, filled with storage tanks and flare stacks, and it has a certain odour. "There's Suncor," I say, pointing ahead. My dad works for the same company in Fort McMurray! Weird, I never knew there was oil in Sarnia."

Peyton's jaw drops. "Mel, are you serious?"

"Yeah, why?"

"Duh . . . the crude oil travels from Alberta to Sarnia by pipeline. The refinery here separates that crude into things like oil and gasoline. You live in Sarnia and you don't know that?"

"Well, so-o-rry! I didn't grow up here."

We turn onto Tashmoo Road and drive past the sign: Welcome to Aamjiwnaang First Nation. Chippewas of Sarnia. Then we go past the office building with the low, brown roof that rises into the shape of a teepee.

"Cool architecture," Peyton notes.

The reserve reminds me of my old subdivision, only the lots are bigger and many have a forest behind them. We pass a split-level home made of brick and vinyl siding. I sigh, thinking of my own home: the one rented by another family for the year. I can't wait until I can move back into my Caribbean blue bedroom and sleep with Chevy again.

Dustin's place stands out from the rest. It's an emerald green bungalow. In the backyard is a tree fort with a rope ladder. Dustin told me he spent a lot of time there when he was younger. Now his six-year-old sister, Kyla, has converted it into a hospital where she treats stuffed animals.

When Peyton drops me off, I walk up the familiar steps to his home. Mrs. Williams greets me at the door with a hug. Kyla runs up and jumps on me. "Melly-Belly, where have you been? I've missed you."

"I've missed you too," I say, tweaking her nose.

"Wanna see my new fish? His name is Jaws and I'm teaching him to play games."

"Wow! What kind of fish is it?"

"An expensive one," she says, her eyes twinkling. "A goldfish."

"Kyla!" her mother calls. "Come here. I need help with something. You can visit Mel later."

When Dustin and I are alone, we sit at the kitchen table. There is still an awkward tension between us. "That was messed up the other night," I say, in an effort to break the ice. "Are you okay?"

Clasping his hands on the table, he stares at me. "It's not me I'm worried about."

"I'm f-fine," I try to tell him, but the tears in my eyes give me away.

Dustin gets up and grabs our coats. "Let's go for a walk."

Outside, we plod through the deep snow in the forest behind his house. Except for the crunch of snow under our feet, it is silent. Large trees tower over us, their leafless branches looking stark against the blue sky. Taking deep breaths, I inhale the cold air into my lungs. Without warning, we hit a patch of ice hidden under the snow. My boots slip and I can't catch my balance. Dustin lunges to catch me and we both go down. He falls face-first, and I end up on my butt. Looking at his snow-covered face, I start to laugh.

"Nice catch, Frosty," I say, pulling snow from his hair. He forces a smile, but even a good fall can't get him to lighten up. He keeps looking at me like he's trying to understand.

"I know a place where we can talk," he says, grabbing my hand and pulling me to my feet. He leads me to a massive oak tree that could be straight out of a fairy tale. The trunk is hollowed out on one side, forming a cave. It's barely big enough for the two of us. Protected from the frigid wind, we huddle inside.

"Is it safe?" I ask, knocking on the wooden walls. "There aren't any roots on this side."

"Oaks are strong," he says. "Even damaged, they can survive."

"Wish it were the same with people," I mutter, without thinking.

"It is," he says. "The kids I meet in drug counselling have been through the worst kind of shit, and lots are able to put their lives back together."

Not all, I'm thinking, as I stare out at the snow drifts.

"This guy you're going out with . . . I'm not impressed."

"I don't expect you to understand," I say, hugging my knees, "but it was good at first. I guess you could say he swept me off my feet . . . but there were signs, and I ignored them, like when he said he loved me and gave me a diamond ring. It seemed too much, too fast . . . but I was caught up in the moment."

Dustin tips his head back against the tree, squeezing his eyes hard. What I'm saying is hard for him to hear, but I need to get it out. "When we talked after the party, he said he didn't mean to push me into the wall. But honestly, I don't know."

Dustin's face goes rigid, but he doesn't say a word.

"There's more," I tell him. "Colter wants to

spend every minute of every day with me. When we're not together, he texts me constantly, even in the middle of the night, and he gets angry if I don't respond." I lower my voice. "The thing I can't forgive is how he tried to keep us apart. That was cruel."

Dustin turns and looks deep into my eyes. "Why are you still with him?"

"He's so screwed up; it's not easy to walk away."

"The guy's messing with your head," he says. "I know you want to help him, but you've got to think about yourself."

I don't say anything.

His eyes search mine. "What about us? Are we cool?"

"Yeah," I say, managing a slight smile.

"Good," he says, with a shiver. He stands up and bends his knees a few times. "I don't know about you, but I'm frozen. My feet feel like blocks of ice."

My legs feel stiff as I get up. The cold has sunk deep in my bones.

"The temperature in Fort McMurray dipped down to minus 40 Celsius yesterday," I tell him. "Mom got so cold she bought a balaclava, a hat that completely covers her head and face, leaving little openings for her eyes. A total zero on the fashion scale."

He cups his hands over his ears. "Wish I had one now."

I laugh. "Me too!"

We lean on each other for support as we walk back to his house, laughing at our frozen bodies.

Chapter 15

Making up for lost time, I've scheduled a full day. When Dustin drops me off at the apartment, Peyton's waiting in her van. I pile into the back with four other girls, and we head to the mall.

Shopping used to be more fun when I worked part time at McDonald's and had extra cash. But when my family moved, and there was no one to pick me up after the late shifts, I was forced to quit. Now I'm living on the monthly allowance my parents put in a bank account. So I buy a new pair of volleyball shoes, and then watch the others shop.

The girls discover a big sale at Kristi's Kloset, a boutique-style clothing store — and the place where Gina works. So I'm glad I'm just hanging out. Gina keeps bringing them armloads of expensive clothes and tells them how "stylish" and "trendsetting" they look. Gag me! She's just trying to drain their debit cards. Being near Gina, I'm starting to feel like the shaken can of Pepsi Mr. Passingham was talking about in Art class. If I stick around, I just know I'll explode all over Gina and make a scene in the store. So I step into the hall and window shop until the others are finished.

On Monday, I'm excited to go to school. Sarah and I drop our stuff at our lockers and head straight to the gym to check the volleyball team posting. As we approach, I spot Peyton in front of a small crowd. Her finger is slipping down the list of players on the bulletin board. Something is wrong. By now, she should be doing a Peyton-style victory dance.

Nudging Sarah, I say, "Peyton looks really upset."

"She should have made the team," Sarah says. "She's one of the top players."

Peyton walks over to us, shaking her head in disbelief. "There must be a mistake."

"Your name should be on the list," I tell her.

Our eyes connect and she looks stunned. "My name *is* on the list." She glances at Sarah. "And so is yours."

I point at myself and choke. "Me?"

"You're our best server," Sarah insists. "Peyton's right — it is a mistake. Let's clear it up, right now."

When we arrive at Coach Burns's office, the door is open, and she waves us in. Peyton speaks up first. "Mel's name isn't on the list. We're wondering —"

Coach cuts her off. "I'd like to speak with Mel . . . alone."

When it's just me and Coach, an uneasy silence fills the room. Reaching for her clipboard, she says, "What's the one thing I ask of my players?"

"Commitment."

"Thirty-seven girls tried out for the team, and they all wanted a spot, just as much as you."

"No! I want it more! I-I don't know why you think —"

She stares down at the clipboard. "You were late for one tryout and you missed the final one."

"But . . . I had a note," I say, my voice faltering, "a doctor's appointment."

Her eyes fix on me. "The office walls are thin."

This can't be happening! She overheard Colter and me, and she knows I lied. Nothing I say will change her mind. When I leave the office, Peyton and Sarah rush up to me. By the look on my face, they know how it went.

"I'll talk to Coach later," Peyton assures me.

"Forget it!" I snap. "She knows I lied. I'm such an idiot!"

"It's Colter's fault," Sarah says under her breath.

She's right, to a point, but I never should have let him talk me into skipping the tryout.

The rest of the day, I'm miserable. In Art, I sit next to Dustin and talk about how my life sucks. He tries to cheer me up, but nothing works.

As the week goes on, I recover a little. Sarah tells me about a recreational volleyball league in her church hall. Even though she's super busy, she offers to join with me, and I'm looking forward to spending more time with her.

Wednesday morning, I'm digging through my locker for a yellow highlighter when Dustin walks up. He props his arm on the door. "I've got my dad's truck. Wanna hang out after school?"

"Sure. Wha'cha have in mind?"

"Doesn't matter. We'll figure something out."

After school, we leave together, joking around as if nothing ever changed. We get in the Silverado and Dustin sets the radio to 103.3 The Eagle, the local aboriginal station. I yank the elastic from my hair, letting my hair fall, as we head off down the road, going nowhere. Luke Bryan's song "I Don't Want This Night to End" comes on, and I find myself singing along. I've got my hands up and I'm rocking in his truck, getting carried away with Luke. We come to a stoplight and I feel Dustin's eyes on me. Glancing at the clock, it reads 3:35. OMG . . . just like in the song! Our eyes meet. This is not my imagination — if there had been no Gina and no Colter, we would be together. We both know it. But the song is ending, and so is the moment.

After driving around for a bit, we end up at the apartment. I grab the hot-air popper and make popcorn with grated cheddar cheese. When we're sitting on the couch, Dustin leans over and says, "Guess what? We're getting a puppy."

"I love puppies! When can I meet him — or her?"

"She's eight weeks old. We're picking her up in a couple of days." He holds up his cell and shows me a picture.

"Aww . . . cute . . . she looks like a baby bear."

"Her mom's a chocolate Lab and her dad's a Great Pyrenees. She's going to be big."

"I'm happy for you," I say. "That was so sad when Ally died — cancer at three years old."

"Yeah," he says, "she was a good dog. After that, Kyla set up her animal hospital, and she's been curing stuffed animals ever since."

I start thinking about my own dog, Chevy, and wonder if he's missing me. Dustin tosses a piece of popcorn at me to get my attention. "I broke up with Gina."

"Huh?" We're talking about puppies and he blurts that bombshell?

"Something you said the other day made me realize —"

I cut him off. "Something *I* said? With my lousy record, I'm the last person you should listen to."

"Give yourself a break," he says, tugging my hair. "It was Colter, not you. Besides, you're not the only one to make a mistake. Gina's not the person I thought — not the person I want to be with."

"What do you mean?"

Sinking low in the couch, he stares at the ceiling. "Most of the time, we got along, but there were times . . . like in a restaurant, when she ordered a Diet Coke and the waitress accidently brought a regular Coke. Gina went off on her, really made a scene. Another time, we were at my house, and I left to help Dad carry some wood. When I returned, Gina said she wanted to go to the Coffee Lodge for cheesecake. In the truck, she told me that she and Kyla had been playing hide-and-seek, and that Kyla was still looking for her."

"Yikes, that *is* mean." I hesitate, then just come out with it: "There's something else you should know. Colter and Gina were both in on the scheme to turn you against me."

He eats a couple of handfuls of popcorn, then mutters, "Doesn't surprise me."

Maybe he's not surprised, but I can tell he's hurt.

"Breaking up," I say, frowning. "It's all I've been thinking about. I still haven't figured out how. All I know is, I can't stay with Colter. The last couple of days, when he's been gone, I've felt like I can breathe again. It feels so good."

"When are you going to tell him?" he asks.

"I'll wait until he gets back, and then I'll figure out a good time. Until then, you and I should keep our distance at school. You know he's super jealous."

Dustin folds his arms. "He doesn't scare me. Besides, waiting won't make it easier."

"I'm not going to break up by text," I insist. "I need to do this my way."

"When does he get back?"

"Sunday."

"Good. We've got four days."

Chapter 16

"Did you miss me?"

I respond with a weak nod and a forced smile.

Colter's flight came in last night. I had hoped to avoid him by arriving at school early and heading straight to class, but he was already at my locker, waiting. The orange T-shirt he's wearing shows off his tan, and the sun has highlighted his hair. Grabbing me in a tight embrace, he kisses me on the lips. I push him away.

"What gives?" he asks, standing back and eyeing me. "I'm gone for a week and this is how you greet me?"

"It's just . . . you know . . . not in front of everyone."

He shoves his hands in his pockets "Since when do you care what others think?"

It's only been a few minutes, and already he's sensing something's wrong. Last night, I put the ring back on my finger, and I'm trying to act normal. But I can't fake it. I've got to do this. But how . . . when? Obviously, not at my locker.

"I'm just in a bad mood," I tell him. "I didn't make the volleyball team."

"Oh . . . that sucks," he says, but I notice he's smiling. "Now we'll be able to spend more time together."

That's it! I'm telling him at lunch.

During my morning classes, I practise what I'm going to say: *You're a great guy but . . . I can't be what you want . . . It's me, not you (actually, it is you!) . . . I'm a closet lesbian . . .*

By lunch, I'm a wreck. We get in his car and drive to Paddy's, a restaurant by the Sarnia Bay. We share an order of potato skins and chicken wings. While we eat, he tells me about the Florida pelicans — how some arrive with fishing lines wrapped around their legs and wings. In other cases, the birds have hooks lodged in their wings or ripping open their pouches. Colter helped feed the ones that were unable to eat on their own. This is even harder than I thought. How can I break up with a guy who helps pelicans?

When we get back to school, I'm leaving for class when Colter calls out, "Meet me after school."

I immediately text Dustin. "help!!"

He's got his dad's truck again and agrees to meet me after last period. Somehow, I have to ditch Colter, which is never simple. When I walk into Art class, he does a little drum roll on the table to announce my arrival. Sitting next to him, I work up to a pout. "I can't hang out today. Aunt Stella arranged for us to have a pedicure. Maybe she's feeling guilty for ignoring me."

"No problem. I've got stuff to do anyway." That's not the reply I expect from him, but I'm glad he's making it easy.

Mr. Passingham gets the class's attention: "Listen up! Today's art assignment is to write five hundred words explaining a quote by the famous Spanish painter, Picasso. 'Art is a lie that makes us realize the truth.'"

A flock of hands start waving in the air.

Mr. Passingham ignores them. "That's all I'm going to say. How you interpret the statement is up to you. Picasso believed in freedom of thought."

I'm not exactly sure what Mr. Passingham just said, but "freedom of thought" sounds like something he won't mark — my favourite kind of assignment.

I glance over at Dustin, catching his attention. His dark eyes crinkle and he's smiling. It's been so long, I can't help myself: I smile back, a big goofy one, and then cringe, hoping Colter didn't see me. The room is starting to close in. Dustin and Colter in the same class is too much. Lowering my head, I get down to work.

At the end of the day, I sneak around the side of the school to meet Dustin. Before we leave, we check to make sure the Mazda is gone.

"I'm hungry," Dustin says as we cross the parking lot. "Let's go to Tim's."

When we arrive, the place is crowded, but we manage to find a table for two by the window. I'm sipping a cappuccino. Dustin is working on his second Canadian Maple doughnut, waiting for me to explain my urgent text.

"I need your help," I say. "I don't know how to break up with him. I know he's going to make it hard . . . more like impossible."

He grunts. "Why are you asking me?"

"You're a guy."

He pops the rest of his doughnut in his mouth, and thinks about it. "Make it short," he says. "Don't try and talk it out. It won't work with a guy like that. I've met a lot of kids at the counselling centre. My job is to hang with them and we talk about everything. I've learned there are people that screw with your head. They'll say anything to get what they want."

"But the stuff he's dealing with is really tough — especially the car accident."

"You're not a shrink. You can't fix him."

I drop my voice to a whisper. "What if he does something crazy?"

"You aren't responsible for him."

When I don't say anything, he tells me about last night's Leafs game — how they scored a short-handed goal in a breakaway and tied the game in the last thirty seconds to force overtime . . . yadda yadda. Lost in my own thoughts, I let him ramble on, his words drifting past my ears.

Dustin can't stay long. His father represents the Aamjiwnaang First Nation on the local environmental advisory board. Dustin has to pick him up from a community meeting about pollution in the St. Clair River. Before we get in the Silverado, he hugs me, and tells me everything will be alright. As he's walking around to the driver's side, he pauses, staring down the road. "Pretty sure that was your boyfriend's car."

I duck down, pressing myself into the side of the truck, trying to make myself invisible.

"Oh, man," Dustin says, shaking his head. "Now he's stalking you."

"Are you sure it was him?" I ask, still crouching.

"It was a silver Mazda and it drove by slowly . . . but I couldn't tell for sure."

"Colter left the school before we did," I remind him. "How could he know? It must be someone else."

"Maybe," he says, but he doesn't sound convinced.

Dustin drops me off in front of the apartment building. I'm walking past a tall evergreen hedge when someone steps out in front of me. I scream, startling an old man. He drops the bag of groceries from his hands. Apologizing, I run after two oranges rolling down the sidewalk.

Get a grip, I tell myself.

A little farther along, I hear a car creeping up behind me. I glance out of the corner of my eye, but can't see anything. Too afraid to turn, I start walking faster toward the entrance.

"What's your hurry?"

Whirling around, I come face to face with Colter. He's drumming his fingers on the steering wheel. The corners of his lips are turned up, although I wouldn't call it a smile. I try, but I can't read his expression.

"Oh, hey," I say, trying to sound normal, even though I'm jumping out of my skin. "Aunt Stella stood me up. Figures. Anyway, I ran into Dustin and he dropped me off."

"Hop in," he says.

My instincts warn me not to get in his car. "Let's go to my place," I suggest. In the elevator, I'm careful to mention that Aunt Stella could be home at any minute. Then I summon up the courage to ask, "How did you know I was here?"

"Just driving around when I saw you," he says.

Creepy, I'm thinking. *What are the chances?*

We sit down in the living room and talk about stuff: like the meaning of the Picasso quote and how he was one of the world's most famous artists, yet he lived in poverty for years. Then Colter mentions Valentine's Day and hints at a surprise he's got for me. He doesn't mention Dustin, and I start to relax, thinking I panicked for nothing. He takes a small box out of his coat pocket and hands it to me. "Got you this in Florida."

I shouldn't accept his present when I'm about to break up with him, but I'm on edge — this whole situation has got me freaked. So I open it and bring out a shell necklace. "It's beautiful."

I'm about to put it on the table, when he grabs it from my hands. "I want to see it on you." He fastens it around my neck, and next thing I know, he's kissing me. His lips are rough, pressing hard against mine. I try pulling away, but he grabs me, pushing me down on the couch . . . holding me so I can't move.

"Stop! You're hurting me!"

His weight pins me to the couch and his hands start moving under my shirt. I'm struggling, but can't break free. The shells in the necklace are digging into my neck, choking me. "I-I can't breathe . . . the necklace!"

"Bitch!" He gets off me. He's breathing hard and his eyes are glazed. He seems to be looking through me, not at me. That's when I realize he did see us! This is his revenge.

Fumbling with my fingers, I manage to unclasp the necklace. Before he can react, I run to the washroom. "Gotta pee," I call. Locking the door, I pull my cell from my jeans and text Peyton.

"Colter's acting crazy need help hurrrrrry"

"on my way"

Stay calm, I tell myself. *You can do this.*

But it's hard to stay calm when he starts banging on the bathroom door. "What's taking so long?"

"I'm brushing my hair," I answer, stalling for time.

The thought of his touch revolts me. As soon

as Peyton arrives, I'm telling him it's over. If he goes berserk, I'll have her for backup. Taking a deep breath, I unlock the door and walk straight to the kitchen. "Just grabbing some water," I say. "My throat's dry." I return holding a bag of chips. He seems to have cooled down a bit, and I need to waste some time, so I hold out the bag. "Want some? They're a new flavour, Cheesy Garlic."

He grabs my other hand. "Tell me that you love me."

I give him a blank stare.

"Say it!" he orders.

I yank my arm away. "I-I can't."

"Don't look away from me," he warns. His eyes are glazing over again, and I can tell he's about to lose it. The chips fall from my hand. I back up slowly, then turn and run for the door. He grabs me, pushing me against the wall, pressing his face into mine. "If you can't say it, then show me. Come on, let's see what Dustin's whore's got."

His mouth digs deep, past my lips, until his teeth mash against mine. I'm trying, but I can't fight him off. The buzzer rings, distracting him, and giving me a chance to lunge for the button that will let Peyton in the building. He grabs my arm, pulling me back. "Don't answer."

"I-I have to," I cry. "It could be important." I'm kicking and punching as he wrestles me to the floor, but in the end, he's stronger.

"Why are you making me do this?" he moans, as if he doesn't have a choice. His words send an eerie chill through me. I feel like I've just glimpsed at the depth of his dark soul.

The lock on the front door turns. Aunt Stella walks in and Peyton rushes up behind her.

Colter gets up and grabs his coat. He leaves without a word.

Aunt Stella is my hero until she opens her mouth. "Sorry, kiddo, bad timing. Looks like things were heating up in here. Next time why don't you hang a 'Do Not Disturb' sign on the door."

Laughing, she heads to the kitchen. It's a new low for my aunt.

Peyton stays overnight so I don't have to be alone. She helps me compose a text to Colter.

"It's over. NEVER contact me again."

Colter's visit was good for something: it made breaking up an easy six-word text.

Chapter 17

The next morning, I'm in line at the cafeteria for breakfast when Sarah runs up and pulls me aside.

"It's Colter," she says, gasping for breath. "He broke into Dustin's locker and put something inside. I've been looking everywhere for Dustin."

My hunger pangs vanish. "Tell me exactly what you saw."

"It was early and the halls were empty," she says, talking fast. "I was in the English classroom, dropping off an assignment. I was about to leave when I saw Colter walking down the hall. After what he did to you last night, I didn't want to go near him, so I waited by the edge of the door. From there, I saw him hanging around Dustin's locker, checking up and down the hall. It seemed strange that he was carrying a brown lunch bag since he never eats at school. When he opened Dustin's locker and placed the bag inside, I knew something was wrong."

"Oh no!" My heart is pounding. "We've got to warn Dustin."

Grabbing my cell, I call him, but it goes to voice mail. All I can do is leave a message.

Turning back to Sarah, I say, "What do you think it was?"

She shrugs. "Maybe a warning — dog poop or a severed finger."

I raise my eyebrows at her.

She laughs at herself. "I read a lot of thrillers."

As we're heading to the second-floor lockers to look for Dustin, Sarah says, "Colter had no problem opening the locker. How did he know the combination? Those two aren't exactly friends."

My heart sinks as I realize he must have found the combination in my art binder.

Suddenly, Sarah grabs my arm and squeezes hard. "He's coming!"

My eyes scan the crowded hallway until I pick him out. He's wearing a brown sweater and jeans. "This way," I say, ducking into one of the wings.

A few seconds later, we return and peer down the hall. Colter's ahead of us now, so I am able to keep an eye on him. The morning bell rings and still no sign of Dustin. Why didn't he return my call? Sarah leaves for class, but I continue in a different direction, tracking Colter. As long as I'm tangled up in the morning rush, it's easy to keep out of sight. But as the crowd starts to thin, I have to be careful.

It quickly becomes obvious Colter is not

heading to class. I follow him to the pay phone inside the main entrance, where he makes a call. That's strange, since he always uses his cell. Realizing this might be my only chance, I turn and take off running. By the time I reach Dustin's locker, the halls are empty. My fingers won't stop trembling as I struggle with the combination. I go through the number sequence, yank, and nothing. Try again, yank — wrong again.

Forcing my fingers to slow down, I try a third time. Finally, I feel the lock release. And there, sitting on the shelf, is his cell. He never got my message!

Dustin's locker is jammed with stuff — books and binders, his wrestling clothes, and something surprising: a picture of me. On the floor, along with his boots and running shoes, I find granola wrappers and a rotten banana peel. No lunch bag. I'm taking too much time. Colter could come along any second.

I'm about to shut the locker when something catches my eye. I kneel down, only to discover more garbage. At the same time, I catch a glimpse of something stuffed in a boot. That must be it! I hesitate, wondering how far Colter would go.

The lunch bag feels weightless. Peering inside, I find little white pills. They resemble aspirin, but I'm betting they're oxycodone. It doesn't take long to add things up in my head. If I'm right, Colter's phone call was to the police and they're on their way now. I can't leave the drugs in Dustin's locker.

As I walk away, I'm feeling like a criminal. And I will be, if I get caught holding this bag. I'm about to toss it in the garbage when a teacher comes around the corner.

"Why aren't you in class?" she asks. "Do you have a late slip?"

Stunned, I hold up the bag. "I — uh — have to put my lunch in my locker and get my books."

She stands there, watching me, as I head to my locker. I have no choice but to put the bag inside. Grabbing my biology binder and pencil case, I head to the office. Not long ago, a late detention was my biggest worry. Now it seems like a joke.

In Biology, I sit at my desk, keeping my eyes trained out the window in the door. Colter is trying to destroy Dustin — because of me! If the police found drugs in his locker, they could charge him with possession. It goes without saying that Mrs. Franklin would expel him from Meridian High. This is the guy who volunteers at a youth drug centre and whose dream is to go to university to become a counsellor.

If I am right, the police will arrive soon. Mrs. Franklin will haul Dustin down to his locker. He will have no idea what's going on. The police will ask him to open it. All they will find is a big mess. Then what? Will they let him go or . . . will they keep searching? Suddenly, I break into a cold sweat. What if they bring in the drug dogs and search the entire school? Can dogs smell oxy? My head falls into my hands. If they can, I'm screwed.

Soon, I hear footsteps in the hall. Two cops walk by. The window in the classroom door is small and high, so I can't see if they've brought the dogs. Sitting there, feeling helpless, I bite my thumbnail down to the skin, and then start on the next finger. For the next twenty minutes, I'm trapped in the classroom, not knowing what's happening.

When Biology is over, I rush into the hall. Everyone is talking, but no one knows anything. Peyton runs up to me, and I can tell she's upset. "Mrs. Franklin and the police came to Math class. They took Dustin. I don't know why."

I pull her close. "Colter set him up."

"No-o-o!" She stares at me in disbelief.

"Don't breathe a word to anyone," I warn, under my breath. "I think I've fixed it . . . I'll explain at lunch."

She's leaving for her next class when I call out, "Wait! Did they bring the dogs?"

"Don't know," she says, with a shrug. "I didn't see any."

Whew! I take that as a good sign.

At lunch, I find Dustin hunched over the table staring at, but not eating, his sandwich. "Hey," I say, walking up. "I heard."

He grunts.

"It'll be okay," I assure him.

His dark eyes narrow. He gives me a long, questioning stare. "How do you know?"

"Cuz you would never —"

"The police searched my locker for drugs.

Mrs. Franklin doesn't believe me when I say I don't know anything. She keeps insisting. 'Where there's smoke, there's fire.'"

I put my hand on his shoulder. "Meet me after school . . . the main entrance."

"Got other plans," he mumbles.

"Drop them," I say firmly.

He looks up at me, his eyes searching. "What's this about?"

"Later," I say, walking away. "There's something I have to do."

Heading to my lunch table, I grab Peyton. We find a quiet place in the hall and I tell her everything, swearing her to secrecy.

"Oh, wow," she says. "If Sarah and you hadn't . . ."

I nod grimly. "One minute later, and she'd have missed the whole thing. If the police had arrested Dustin, how would he defend himself? Who would believe him? Certainly not Mrs. Franklin."

"Dustin needs to know," she insists. "He's a wreck."

"I'm telling him after school. If he finds out now, he'll go after Colter. Then Mrs. F will have another reason to expel him."

"She doesn't know?" Peyton exclaims. "Mel, you have to report it! Colter can't get away with this."

I shake my head firmly. "I can hear Mrs. F now. 'Miss Rankin, you withheld information and you tampered with a drug scene. You are just as much a criminal as Dustin.'"

"But Sarah would back you up," Peyton insists.

"And then, she'd get in trouble too . . . for reporting the incident to me, instead of the office." I pause, thinking. "We'll go to the police and tell them everything. Dustin's meeting me at the front entrance after school. I need you and Sarah there too."

Peyton gives me a hug. "You're being so brave."

"No, I'm terrified. But I need to do this for Dustin . . . and for me. Once the truth comes out, Colter will get kicked out of Meridian. I don't ever want to see him again."

"That makes two of us," she says, high-fiving me.

All afternoon, I'm dreading Art class. The thought of being in the same room with Colter makes me sick. When he doesn't show, I am majorly relieved. Sitting next to Dustin, I get straight to work. We're painting a typical still life: a bowl of fruit.

Dustin's in a really bad mood. We don't talk, and that's fine with me. Right now, talk is dangerous.

Mr. Passingham gives a short lecture on blending watercolours. When he finishes, Dustin turns to me and pins me down with his stare. "You know something."

"Yes," I admit.

"Tell me."

"Not here. After school."

"Now." There's a cold anger in his voice. He's looking at me like I'm the enemy.

I glance up at the clock. "Thirty minutes, and then I'll tell you what I know. Promise."

Growling, he returns to his work.

Chapter 18

After class, I hurry to my locker, stuff the lunch bag in my backpack, grab my coat, and then head outside. I arrive before the others and wait by the school bus zone. Big flakes of snow are falling. It's nice — not too cold. Inhaling the fresh air feels good. I know I'm doing the right thing by going to the police. Now I just want to get it over with.

A school bus rolls up, slowly chugging past me. And then another. They conceal the car behind them. *Geez . . . can't I ever catch a break?* As Colter pulls up beside me, I'm wishing I could disappear. What is he doing here? When he didn't show up for last period, I figured he'd gone home to celebrate.

"Hey!" he calls to me, smiling like nothing's happened. "Let's talk. I don't understand why you want to break up."

"There's nothing to talk about," I say, my voice trembling with rage. Reaching in my backpack, I take a step toward his car, dangling the lunch bag in front of him. "By the way, your plan backfired. You won't get away with it."

His smile disappears. "We'll see about that. My dad's a really good lawyer."

I start to walk away, then spin back. "Why Dustin? He didn't do anything."

"Oh, yeah? It didn't look that way yesterday when I saw you in each other's arms.

"He's not the problem!" I cry. "You are."

He shrugs. "Then get in. Let's talk about it."

"No!" I'm half crying, half yelling by this point.

He leans across the front seat. "Do you want me to back off Dustin?"

I nod mutely.

"Then quit waving the bag of drugs in the air like you want to get busted and get in."

Glancing around the parking lot, I say, "My friends are meeting me here any minute now."

"Give me two minutes," he says. "Hey, I get it. It's over. All I want is an explanation, and then I'll leave you alone."

More than anything I want him out of my life. "Fine," I say, getting in and staring out the windshield.

He swivels my head around to face him. "I gave you everything. All I wanted was to make you happy."

"You attacked me!" I cry. "And you tried to destroy Dustin. How could that possibly make me happy?"

He lowers his head onto the steering wheel. "I was trying to show you that I love you."

"Rape is not love," I snarl.

His head shoots up, and he glares at me. "You think you can just leave me . . . that I'm going to make it easy?"

"Stay out of my life," I warn. "Dustin's too."

"Don't order me around."

"We're done," I say, reaching for the door handle. At the same time, I hear a whirring sound and a click. The windows are closing and the door won't open. I try to unlock it, but can't. The windows don't work either. That's when I realize he's used the childproof locks. "Let me out!" I scream.

He grabs my arm, pulling me toward him. "We're done when I say we're done."

"Let me go!" I insist, struggling to break his grip.

"You act all innocent, but this is your fault. You led me on — made me believe you cared. You're just like the rest."

Just then, I see Peyton and Dustin walking out of the school. Sarah is a couple of steps behind. They're glancing around, looking for me. I'm so close — a few metres away, partially hidden behind the next bus. While I'm distracted, Colter snatches the lunch bag from beside me.

"Know what I really want?" he says, coldly. "To feel no pain." He pops a couple of pills in his mouth. "If you chew 'em, you get a better high."

Shocked, I turn and face him. "Why would you

do that? You've seen what they've done to your father."

"As . . . if . . . you . . . care."

Grabbing my cell from my pocket, I start to text. Before I can press send, he knocks it from my hand. Desperate, I start banging on the closed window. "Help!"

All of a sudden, Dustin looks over and sees me. He comes running and lunges at the car, trying to open the door. When he can't get in, he bangs his fists on the hood.

"Get your hands off my car!" Colter yells. Without warning, he turns on the ignition. Wrenching the steering wheel, he accelerates away from the curb.

"Stop!" I grab for the keys to cut the ignition. He pushes me back forcefully. I'm afraid if I try anything else, we might crash. That's when I secure my seatbelt. He clutches the wheel hard, staring ahead, accelerating.

"You're scaring me!" I cry. "Slow down."

He's driving seventy kilometres in a fifty-k zone, and still accelerating. I grab the passenger handle, holding on for dear life. I beg him to pull over. Ignoring me, he races down the street, past rows of homes in a quiet subdivision. At first, the road feels greasy with wet snow, but suddenly and without warning, we hit a patch of ice. The car starts sliding out of control. Next thing I know, we're spinning, doing 360s toward a parked car. I brace myself for impact. Then, at the last second,

I feel the tires catch in the snow. Colter pulls out of the skid and the car comes to a stop facing the wrong way on the road.

"What a rush!" he exclaims, pumping his fist in the air. "Love those ABS brakes!"

"You could have killed us!" I grab the door handle. "You've had your fun, now let me out."

"Not so fast." His voice rises with sick pleasure. "Here comes the rescue squad. What do you say we have some real fun?"

Dustin's truck is coming around the corner. Peyton is sitting in the front seat next to him. Sarah is in the back, leaning forward so she can see out the windshield.

I grab his arm. "Please, Colter, I want out."

"Sure, Mel, whatever you say." He revs the engine, turns the car around, and takes off again. "When I'm ready."

I grip the seat. "Are you trying to scare me . . . or kill me? What is it?"

He looks at me with wild staring eyes. "Let's just say, I'm teaching you a lesson . . . like I did with Jillian."

"Jillian? Oh my god, the accident — it wasn't an accident. What did you do?"

"She . . . wouldn't . . . listen . . . to me," he says in cold, measured words, "wouldn't . . . stay . . . away . . . from him."

I close my eyes, sobbing silently.

He races down Lakeshore Road, weaving around slower cars. Dustin is smart enough not to ride on his tail. He keeps his distance, but it's still dangerous on the slippery roads.

Colter is closing in on a hundred kilometres along a straight stretch of road, speeding toward Bright's Grove, a small community on the outskirts of the city. He's driving way too fast as we approach the S-curve in the road. As we enter the curve, I feel the car losing traction — the back end is sliding over the centre line. Colter tries to correct, pulling the steering wheel too hard and sending us skidding toward the ditch. A blue van is coming in the other direction — a woman and young child are sitting in the front seat. I see the terror in the woman's eyes as she swerves to avoid us. We hit hard, the driver's side smashing into the back of the van. A deafening explosion goes off in my ears as my body hits the air bag. Just as quickly, I'm flung backward as the car spins off the road and down into the ditch.

Chapter 19

How long has it been? I'm staring out the broken windshield at the trees. They are tilting on angles. Snow is gently falling. Each flake makes its own unique pattern. I learned that somewhere — in kindergarten, I think. Looking outside, the world seems so peaceful.

I try to move my leg, but it hurts — a sharp, stabbing pain. Warm, salty liquid is trickling into my mouth. The accident is coming back, but I'm confused. Time and space feel strangely altered. I glance over at Colter. He's slumped forward in his seat, not moving. Blood is seeping from his head. I observe this, but I don't react.

Suddenly, I hear something, a voice from outside. "Are you okay?"

Dustin's hand reaches through the broken window on the driver's side. He flips the locks, then rushes around and opens my door. "Can you move?" He reconsiders. "Maybe you shouldn't . . . something could be broken."

"I'm okay." I start to get out, unaware the car is tipped on an angle in the ditch. There's no ground under my feet. But Dustin's there, catching me before I fall. I try to walk on my own, but I'm limping. My leg is in terrible pain.

"Colter . . . is he dead?"

Dustin shrugs. "The driver's side got smashed badly. The fire department will be here any minute, and they'll be able to get him out safely."

Draping his jacket around me, he holds me tight. Even so, my teeth won't stop chattering.

Peyton comes running from the road. She looks completely freaked. "Mel, are you okay? Your nose is bleeding."

I touch my face. "Oh . . . yeah, my whole head hurts."

She whispers something to Dustin and he tells her, "We're fine. You go."

"Where's she going?" I ask. "And where's Sarah?"

"They're helping the people in the van."

"What van?" I catch my breath, suddenly remembering. "Are they alright?" Before he can answer, I grab onto him, feeling like I might faint.

Scooping me in his arms, he carries me to the road. Two fire trucks and a police car have arrived. An officer is busy blocking off the area. In the distance, I hear the high shriek of ambulance sirens. Suddenly, I see the van. It's really smashed up, the entire back end is crushed.

Dustin places me in his truck and turns up the heat. "Don't move," he orders. "I'll get help."

Now I'm alone and crying. I don't want to believe any of this. Closing my eyes, I try to make it go away. Before long, the truck door is opening and a woman in uniform is smiling at me. "Hi, I'm a paramedic. I'm here to help you."

My eyes shift to the scene behind her. I see a small body on a stretcher.

"No!" I cry. "Not the little girl!"

Suddenly, everything comes into sharp focus, and it feels real and ugly. And I can't stop myself: I'm screaming hysterically.

***

The hospital is a noisy place at night with clanking carts and strange voices in the halls, loud alarms and ringing phones. I'm sharing a room with a woman who moaned all night. She doesn't speak to me, just moans. I feel bad for her, but at the same time, she scares me.

Over the past twelve hours, I've had a pile of tests. Turns out, I have a cracked tibia (that's the medical name for shin bone), and I'll be in a cast for six weeks. My face is scraped, my brain's rattled, and my ears are ringing from the explosion of the air bag. The doctor explained I was suffering from psychological shock after the accident, which is why I was acting odd. A severe trauma can do that. They gave me pills to calm me down.

Considering everything, I'm feeling surprisingly strong. Maybe it's the effect of the drugs, but I don't think so. A couple of things have got me feeling pretty happy. The little girl in the accident made it through her surgery okay. And late last night, Mom and Dad flew in from Fort McMurray. Right now, they're out getting me a burger and fries. My wildflower picture, the one I tossed in the recycling bin, is on the night table. Dustin must have saved it that day. Sweet! Guess he dropped by my room when I was in X-ray.

While I'm trying to figure out how the hospital phone works, a man dressed in a suit arrives, holding a bouquet of flowers and a box of chocolates. I figure he's visiting the lady in the next bed. Goodness knows, she needs cheering up. But he walks past her and hands the gifts to me. "You must be Mel," he says, with a big smile. "I'm Colter's dad."

Every muscle tightens, flooding fresh pain through my body. I don't want to think about Colter. It's too hard, too fresh in my mind.

"Just checking to see how you're doing," he says.

"Fine," I reply, wishing him away.

No such luck. He pulls up a chair and sits. "Colter's having a rough time," he tells me. "After the accident, they transported him to the critical care unit in London. The doctors are working to keep the swelling in his brain down." He bows his head.

"Overnight . . . it got pretty scary, but he's out of danger now. I was able to speak to him this morning, but only briefly."

"That's good," I say quietly.

"My son is a good kid. It's just that he's emotional, easily upset," he goes on. "He's broken up over the way things turned out between you two, and he'd love a chance to make things right." He pauses, waiting for my response. When it doesn't come, his expression darkens. "Listen, I'm trying to piece this thing together. Perhaps you could help me with something? The police said they found drugs in the car. Do you know how they got there? You see, that could be important in the outcome of this case — if, indeed, there *is* a case."

I know what he's implying and I don't say a word.

"Smart girl," he says. "You have to be careful what you say . . . and to whom: the police, for example. If you press charges, it just might come back and bite you." He runs his fingers through his greying hair and smiles. "So tell me, how can I help?"

I sit up in bed, suddenly realizing there is something he can do. "Keep Colter away from me and from Dustin Williams."

His lips tighten. "You're angry now. When Colter's feeling better, you two need to talk."

"No."

"Okay," he says, sighing. "I'll do my best."

Lying back on my bed, I tell Mr. Wagner I'm

feeling tired, meaning . . . leave. When he's halfway out the door, I call him back. "There's something else!" I say. "I want you to send Pixie to Florida."

His eyes turn cold and menacing. "That's an odd request and an expensive one."

Yanking the ring off my finger, I toss it to him. "This will cover the expenses."

"Hmmph . . . never did like that dog," he mutters, but he agrees. He thinks he's bought me off, but he's wrong. I won't let Colter walk away from this.

Mom and Dad arrive shortly with the burger and fries. Before Mom can sit, I ask her to take the flowers and the chocolates to the little girl down the hall. I believe this is the first time I've ever refused chocolate.

Later in the day, the doctor discharges me from the hospital. Before I am able to leave, Dad hurries off to buy me crutches. Mom sits on the edge of my bed, looking tired.

"We can't do this anymore," she says, stroking my hair. "Your dad and I have made a decision. I'm quitting my job and moving back to Sarnia. Dad will stay in Fort McMurray until we save some money and I can find a job here. Lori will stay with Dad and finish off the school year." She ruffles my hair. "See? We've got it all figured out."

"Huh?" I say, stunned. "What will you do? Move in with Aunt Stella?"

"If she'll let me."

"Mom, I was kidding! We'd have to share the bedroom."

"It would only be for a short while," she explains. "Now that I have some experience, getting a job should be easier."

Sitting up in the bed, I point out, "You quit your old job and went back to school to find a career that makes you happy. Every time we talk, you tell me about the important work you're doing in the oil sands. You should finish the contract."

"It's not the same without you," she says, tears welling up in her eyes. "In just over a year, you'll be leaving us, going off to school somewhere. I don't want to miss this time. You are more important to me than the job."

After living with Aunt Stella and feeling like an orphan, her words fill a vacant pit inside me. But I don't tell her — I don't want her to know how hard it's been.

Our conversation gets interrupted when Dad arrives with the crutches. He gives me a quick lesson, then hands them to me, saying, "Have a nice trip."

"Very funny," I say, jolting forward and hitting the corner of the door. "Ouch!"

The next day, I'm in Aunt Stella's kitchen pouring myself some milk while eavesdropping on the conversation in the living room. Aunt Stella is telling my parents that she had no idea I was in trouble, and she couldn't understand why I didn't ask for help. What a pile of crap! I can't listen. I had been thinking about joining them, but I go on Facebook instead.

At three o'clock, I grab my coat. Still awkward on my crutches, I manage to get down the elevator and wait at the front entrance. Dustin just texted me saying he's left the school, and he can't wait for me to meet his new puppy. He has no idea that I am about to ruin his day.

Chapter 20

"Mmmm . . . wet puppy kisses. I wuv, wuv, wuv you to pieces."

The Williams's new puppy, Maddy, is wiggling in my arms, giving my face a bath with her tongue. When I put her down, she starts running in circles and then chews on my crutches. What a cutie-pie! After we've played on the floor for a while, Kyla and her parents take her to show the neighbours. Dustin and I sit on the couch. I elevate my leg on a stool: doctor's orders for the next few days. The glowing embers in the woodstove make the room feel warm and cozy. Up until now, Dustin's been teasing me about my odd behaviour after the accident. But now, he's looking at me with concern. "Are you okay?"

"Yes, Dr. Phil."

He yanks my ponytail. "Quit kidding. You've been through a lot."

"I don't want to talk about it. Not yet. But thanks for coming after me in your truck. I was so scared. Knowing you were there helped."

"I was scared too," he says softly. "Not for me . . . for you."

We sit there, staring into the flames. Dustin's foot is tapping the air like machine gun fire. He's geared up about something. Clearing his throat, he turns to me and says, "I never got over you."

"What?" I don't know if I should hug him or hit him with my crutch. Those words could have changed everything. None of this would have happened. Now it's too late.

"When you wouldn't go out with me, I tried to forget you," he says. "I thought going out with Gina would help. It didn't."

I stare at him in disbelief. "Seriously, Dustin, couldn't you tell that I liked you? I followed you around like a friggin' groupie."

Our eyes meet and he groans. "Why didn't you say something? Kiss me . . . anything? Watching you and Colter together drove me a nuts." He pauses, searching my eyes. "So now, I'm telling you. I'm crazy about you. We've spent a lot of time together and we know each other well, both the good and the bad."

This time, I do hit him with my crutch. "What bad stuff?"

"You know what I mean," he says, trying to be serious.

"Hmmm," I say. "Like when you yank my

ponytail to get my attention, or order onions on your pizza, and go on and on about the Leafs — as if I care?"

"Ouch!" He clutches his chest. "I thought you enjoyed my daily updates." He takes a deep breath. "What I'm trying to say is —"

"Stop!" I can't let him go on. The next part is really hard, but he needs to know. "I-I'm moving to Fort McMurray. We're leaving tomorrow. I'll be gone for six months."

He looks away, stunned. "Don't let him drive you away."

"I don't want to be looking over my shoulder, expecting to see him," I say. "Besides, I miss my family and I can't wait to snowboard some real mountains."

He glances down at my cast and frowns. "Are you sure it's what you want?"

I nod, biting my bottom lip. "It was my decision."

"Then I'll wait for you."

"We're in high school," I remind him, "too young to be hung up in a long-distance relationship."

"I tried to move on, remember? When I talked about it with my mom, she said, 'The heart wants what the heart wants.' It's that simple . . . and that difficult." He looks deep into my eyes. "I want you. If you feel the same, we owe it to each other to give this relationship a shot. Six months will go by quickly. Besides, I'll have Maddy to keep me company."

I shrug, struggling with my emotions. After everything that's happened, I don't know if I'm ready for a relationship — even a long-distance one. At the same time, I don't want to lose Dustin again.

"My parents are hoping to move back to Sarnia," I say, being realistic. "But what if they can't find work here? There is no guarantee."

He won't back down. "After everything we've been through, it's just a plane ride. You could visit this summer and I could go out next Christmas. We're both graduating next year. We could apply to the same university. And if you find someone else out there and want to break my heart . . . then at least we tried."

I look at him, considering the possibility. "You'd make a terrible computer boyfriend. You spend all your time on Xbox."

"Hey, that gives me an idea!" he says, his face lighting up. "We could hook up to the Internet and play against each other. Your sister's got an Xbox, right?"

"Are you serious?" I laugh. "Okay . . . maybe."

He smiles. "You mean, maybe you'll be my girlfriend?"

"I mean, maybe I'll play Xbox."

"Good enough," he says, grinning. "It's a start. So . . . what time are you leaving tomorrow?"

"The morning." I swallow hard, knowing this is the last time we'll see each other. "Mom and Dad have to get back to work. Lori and Chevy are staying with a friend until we return. And I have to get ready to start my new school." I grimace. "Not looking forward to that."

"I'll miss you," he says, tears filling his eyes.

"I'll miss you too." We hold each other, neither wanting to let go.

***

Air Canada, Flight 1197, nonstop to Fort McMurray, Alberta, is taxiing down the runway at Toronto Pearson International. The plane is in line behind three others, waiting for takeoff. I'm in the window seat, Mom's sitting next to me, and Dad's in the aisle seat.

Mom turns to me. "The last few days have been such a whirlwind, I forgot to tell you. When I was at Meridian arranging to have your files transferred, I spoke with the principal."

I make a face. "That must have been a treat."

"Mrs. Franklin did raise a good point," she insists. "You never should have taken matters into your own hands. If you had been found in possession of drugs on school property, there could have been serious consequences."

Not in the mood for a lecture, I snap back. "It wasn't just me. I was protecting Dustin and Sarah. You don't know Mrs. Franklin. If I had told her the truth, she would have twisted it around to make us all guilty. Then you would have been coming to Sarnia to bail me out."

Mom tilts her head and frowns. "Mrs. Franklin

knows she let you down and she feels badly. She wants Meridian High to be the kind of place where students feel they can reach out for help. She says she's going to make some changes. Also, she sends her best wishes for a speedy recovery."

"Wow, Mrs. Franklin admitting she's wrong. That's a first."

I turn and look out the window so no one can see the tears in my eyes. I am broken in a million different ways. As much as I want this pain to go away, he's there, infecting my mind, like a disease. When I spoke with the police officer after the accident, she was very interested when I gave her new information about Jillian's death. Despite Mr. Wagner's subtle threats, I am pressing charges, hoping it will force Colter to get help. Otherwise, what's stopping him from charming the next girl? And when she can't live up to his twisted expectations, how far will he go next time?

The plane starts to accelerate, the jet engines are roaring. As we lift off, I'm staring out the window, watching the ground grow smaller, the cars and buildings becoming insignificant, and wishing it were really that easy to leave.